P9-CEY-287

Geronimo Stilton

THE KINGDOM OF FANTASY

Scholastic

New York   Toronto   London   Auckland

Sydney   Mexico City   New Delhi   Hong Kong

ISBN-13: 978-0-545-98025-8
ISBN-10: 0-545-98025-9

Copyright © 2003 by Edizioni Piemme S.p.A., Via Galeotto del Carretto 10, 15033 Casale Monferrato (AL), Italia. International Rights © Atlantyca S.p.A. Via Leopardi 8, 20123 Milan – Italy, foreignrights@atlantyca.it
English translation copyright © 2009 by Atlantyca S.p.A.

Text by Geronimo Stilton
Original title *Nel Regno Della Fantasia*
Cover by Iacopo Bruno and Lorenzo Chiavini
Illustrations by Larry Keys, Topica Topraska, Mary Fontina, Johnny Stracchino, Topilia Aristoratti, and Iacopo Bruno
Graphics by Topea Sha Sha, Zeppola Zap, Toposhiro Toposawa, Soia Topiunchi, Merenguita Gingermouse, and Quesita de la Pampa

Special thanks to Kathryn Cristaldi
Special thanks to Lidia Morson Tramontozzi
Interior composition by Kay Petronio

27 26 25 24 23   18 19 20 21 22/0

Printed in China   38
First printing, October 2009

THE ORDER OF THE FAIRY QUEEN

GERONIMO STILTON: He runs *The Rodent's Gazette*, the most famouse newspaper on Mouse Island. He's a brainy mouse who likes to write about his fabumouse adventures. Now he's on a journey through the Kingdom of Fantasy.

SCRIBBLEHOPPER: This is Geronimo's official guide through the Kingdom of Fantasy. A chatterbox who calls himself a literary frog, he dreams of writing a bestselling book.

SHELLY: This wise, generous turtle is the guide through the Kingdom of the Mermaids. She's got a hard shell, but inside she's all heart.

PRINCESS SCATTERBRAIN: The granddaughter of King Firebreath III. She's the guide through the Kingdom of the Dragons. A bit on the ditzy side, she'll do anything to get out of going to school.

TRICK: Mischievous and playful, he is one of the guides through the Kingdom of the Pixies, but only because King Chuckles ordered him to be!

FACTUAL: The wise and kind King of the Gnomes. He loves to read and is fascinated with all types of sciences. He's always cheerful and knows how to see the positive side of everything.

COZY: The Queen of the Gnomes. She's an excellent cook, an expert gardener, and the one who rules the household!

GIANT: He's forgotten his real name. He's the guide through the Kingdom of the Giants.

BLINKETTE: This tiny, brave firefly is Geronimo's guide through the Kingdom of the Fairies.

IT ALL STARTED
LIKE THIS...

Dear Rodent Friends,

Do you know me? My name is Stilton, *Geronimo Stilton*. I run a newspaper called *The Rodent's Gazette*. It's the most popular paper on Mouse Island. But I'm not here to squeak about the paper. I want to tell you a story that will make your fur stand on end!

It all started like this...

It all started like this exactly like this

Geronimo Stilton

RATS! WHY TODAY, OF ALL DAYS?

It was the morning of June 21,* and I had just set paw in the office. Right away I could tell it wasn't going to be a good day. My staff was running around like a pack of rats in a maze. And everyone was **COMPLAINING** about something.

"Geronimo, the air-conditioner's broken!" yelled my secretary, Mousella MacMouser.

"Geronimo, we're out of **COFFEE**!" shrieked Blasco Tabasco, one of my designers.

"Geronimo, the **COMPUTERS** are all down!" cried my proofreader, Mickey Misprint.

"Geronimo, I want a **RAISE**!" squeaked my assistant editor, Pinky Pick.

"Geronimo, did you know you have a pimple on your snout?" my cousin Trap asked.

*June 21 marks the beginning of summer. Legend has it that the evening of June 21 is a magical night when anything can happen.

The editorial offices of THE RODENT'S GAZETTE

HERE'S WHAT WAS HAPPENING AT *THE RODENT'S GAZETTE*... TODAY, OF ALL DAYS!

1. **Hercule Poirat** wanted to talk about a new case.
2. **Yogi Fur** was practicing standing on his head.
3. **Kreamy O'Cheddar** was spraying perfume on my prize pepper plant.
4. The **architect** was redesigning the office.
5. The **cleaning mouse** was washing the floor.
6. **Thea** was doing wheelies on her new motorcycle.
7. **Blasco Tobasco** was conked out on the couch.
8. **Tina Spicytail** had made an extra-smelly blue cheese pie.
9. **Coral Cockle** had brought over a sack of slimy fish.
10. **Stephanie von Sugarfur** had returned my love letter.
11. The **delivery rat** from the café brought the wrong order.
12. **Penelope Poisonfur** wanted me to go mountain climbing.
13. The **janitor**'s three-year-old niece came to visit.
14. **Professor Paws von Volt** was working on the computer cables.
15. The **water delivery rat** brought saltwater by accident.
16. My uncle **Samuel S. Stingysnout** wanted to talk about the meaning of life.
17. Someone kicked a soccer ball through our window.
18. I, **Geronimo Stilton,** had a pimple on my snout.
19. A **sculptor** was hammering out a bust of my grandfather.
20. An **illustrator** and an **editor** were arguing.
21. **Benjamin** wanted to do his homework in the office.
22. The **technicians** were repairing the air-conditioner.
23. Three hundred and three contracts had to be signed.
24. **Bruce Hyena** brought his new weights to the office.
25. **Pinky Pick** and her uncle **Mousias van Raten** were singing.
26. **Shorty Tao** was practicing karate chops.

Was it true? I grabbed a mirror. Rats! There really was a pimple on my snout. Oh, why did I have to get a pimple **TODAY, OF ALL DAYS**?

What a HUMONGOUS pimple!

After a million hours, the day finally ended. I was exhausted. I headed for home. That's when things went from bad to worse.

I began walking home just as it started raining. Suddenly, a bolt of *lightning* almost hit my tail. My fur stood on end. My teeth chattered. My paws went weak. Oh, why did I almost get struck by lightning, **TODAY, OF ALL DAYS**?!

ZZZt! ZZZZZt! ZZZt!

BOOM! KABOOM! BOOM! KABOOM!

THE LIGHTS GO OUT IN THE ATTIC

At last, I made it home. All of the lights were out. **Cheese niblets!** I'd have to go up to the attic to get the candles.

In the attic, I stepped on my grandma Honeywhisker's rake. It hit me right in the snout. **OUCH!**

My grandmother's rake

My grandfather's bookcase

My cousin's roller skate

I grabbed on to Grandfather William's bookcase. It tumbled down on top of me. **Yikes!**

I rested my paw on my cousin Trap's roller skate and went flying through the air. My head crashed through a portrait of my Dutch ancestor Ludwig van der Stilton.

I ended up with my aunt Sweetfur's little straw hat perched right on top of my head.

"SQUEAK!" I managed to mumble. Then I fainted.

When I came to, it was the middle of the night. I tried to remember what I was doing up in the attic. Then I felt the lump on my head. **OUCH!**

My ancestor's portrait

My aunt's little straw hat

It all came flooding back to me. I had been looking for some **CANDLES**. I opened up the drawer of an old dresser. I found a candlestick and I lit it.

"That's better," I said with a sigh. Did I tell you I'm afraid of the D A R K ?

I looked around the attic. I spotted a bookcase of stories from when I was a young mouselet.

Once upon a time...

My sister Thea's tricycle sat in one corner. I smiled. Even on a tricycle, Thea had been a ***DAREDEVIL***.

An old bedsheet lay in a heap on the floor. It was my cousin Trap's ghost costume from long ago. He used to love to scare me

Vrooooommm!

Booo!

with it. I rolled my eyes. If there's one thing you should know about my cousin, it's that he loves to get under my fur!

Just then, I saw a **SHADOW**. My whiskers stood on end. My heart began to pound. I was so **SCARED** I couldn't even squeak.

Then I noticed something. The shadow was coming from a mannequin propped up against the wall. It had my aunt Sugarfur's *wedding* dress on it. What a nincompoop I was! *Get a grip, Geronimo,* I told myself.

Right at that moment, the attic window burst open. **SLAM!**

THE MYSTERIOUS CRYSTAL MUSIC BOX

I jumped a mile high. Well, OK, maybe not an actual mile, but you get the picture. I reached out to shut the window. The storm was over, and the clouds had cleared. I saw the trail of a **SHOOTING STAR** light up the sky. I was about to make a wish when, suddenly, the star's trail came in through the window! It lit up a **MYstE RIOUs** object at my feet. It was a glittering crystal **music box**.

I scratched my head.

Now how did that get there?

A Delicate Scent of Roses

The music box shone in the candlelight. Precious stones were set into its sides. A ruby, a **topaz**, a citrine, an emerald, a *sapphire*, and an Amethyst. A sparkling DIAMOND was set at the very top of the box. Letters were engraved on the front. They seemed to be part of some strange alphabet.

I raised the lid. The music box was lined with **red** velvet. A scent of sweet roses spread through the room. A melody tinkled softly in the air.

I was starting to feel a little strange. It was as

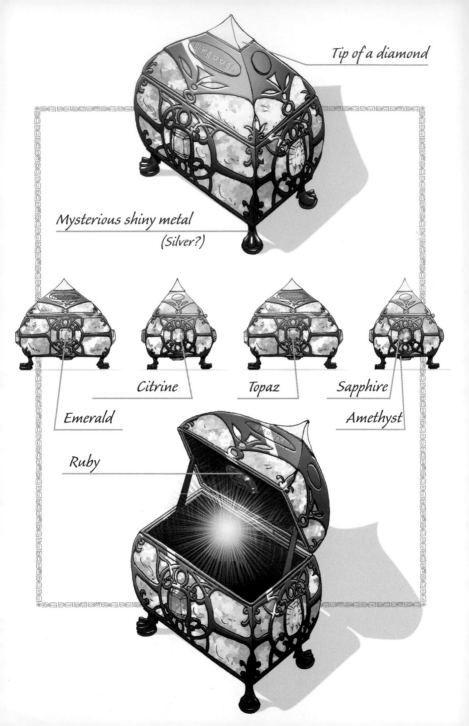

Tip of a diamond

Mysterious shiny metal
(Silver?)

Citrine

Topaz

Sapphire

Emerald

Amethyst

Ruby

if the music box had put me under some sort of magical spell.

For a moment, I thought I saw a tiny beam of light dancing inside the music box. I blinked. I knew I shouldn't have skipped my appointment with Dr. Squinty Snout. I needed new glasses. Then I realized that I wasn't looking at a beam of light. I was looking at a glittering golden key. What was it for?

Next to the key lay a tiny *rose*-colored scroll with a wax seal. Carefully, I unrolled the paper. It contained a mysterious message written in that strange alphabet. How fascinating! I pulled out a magnifying glass to check it out.

A Stairway of Golden Dust

Just then, I heard a rustling noise. I looked up and saw the most amazing sight. The star's trail had turned into a stairway made of golden dust! Far, far away, at the top of the stairs, I could make out a little golden door.

Now let me tell you, I am not the bravest mouse on the block. In fact, I guess you could say I am a bit of a scaredy mouse. Well, OK, I am a total scaredy mouse. But I was curious about that door. I just had to take a look. I packed up a few supplies in my backpack and crept slowly up the stairs.

With my heart in my throat, I crept up...

THE GOLDEN DOOR

My heart hammered under my fur. My paws trembled. At last, I reached the little golden door. These words were inscribed on it:

YOU MUST GO BACK TO BEING SMALL! IF YOU WISH TO ENTER AT ALL!

OK, now I was getting *really scared*. *That's enough excitement for one day,* I decided. But when I turned around to go back, I discovered the golden staircase was disappearing!

Rotten rats' teeth! I tried to open the little door in front of me. It was locked.

Just then, I noticed a tiny keyhole. I took out the golden key and slid it into the keyhole. It worked! I crouched down and walked through the door.

O KNIGHT IN SHINING ARMOR!

I looked around. I was in a crystal cave. What was this place?

My thoughts were interrupted by a croaking voice.

"Good day to you, Fair Knight in Shining Armor!" the voice called. "What wonderful

deed will you perform today?"

I whirled around. That's when I saw him. He had lumpy greenish skin, large **BULGING** eyes, and a double—no, a **TRIPLE CHIN**.

Can you guess what kind of creature I am talking about? Think lily pads, flies, and things that go croak in the night. Yep, he was a *frog*.

But this was no ordinary frog. He was wearing a jacket and vest made of red velvet. He had on green tights and a funny three-pointed hat. I watched as he pulled out a piece of paper from his bag. Then he picked up a *strange* feathered pen and stared at me.

"Let's try this again, shall we?" he said. "O Fair Knight in Shining

Scribblehopper, a Literary Frog

Armor, what wonderful deed will you perform today?"

I chewed my whiskers. **Cheese niblets**, this frog really had me wrong. "My name is Stilton, *Geronimo Stilton*. I'm not a knight. I'm not in shining armor. I'm a mouse," I tried to explain. "And I was in the attic and then the music box, that is, the star, I mean the window. . ."

The frog shook his head. "Sorry, Knight, that just won't work. Your story is too boring. I need something heart-pounding. Something with **sword fights**, *dragons*, and **treasure**," he insisted. "After all, I'm writing a *book* about your adventures. So,  let's see. You call yourself

Sir Geronimo of Stilton, is that right?"

I tried to correct him, but the strange frog wouldn't listen. Instead, he started scribbling away:

Through the Golden Door came a Knight in Shining Armor. Sir Geronimo of Stilton! He was tall, handsome, and mighty, with proud blue eyes and radiant blond fur. He was wearing a suit of silver armor that glimmered in the moonlight, and his invincible sword was . . .

I'm Just an Ordinary Mouse!

What was this crazy frog talking about? I don't have blue eyes. I don't have blond fur. And a suit of armor would CLASH with my tie!

Still, the frog, whose name was Scribblehopper, wouldn't listen. He rambled on and on. Then he pointed at my snout. "How fascinating," he croaked. "I've never met a knight with a pimple before."

I gnashed my teeth together. *Keep your cool, Geronimo,* I told myself. But it wasn't easy. "I AM NOT A KNIGHT!" I squeaked at the top of my lungs. "And leave my pimple alone!"

The frog smirked. "Of course you're a knight," he chuckled. "And I am a Literary Frog. I am writing a bestselling adventure tale and you are

the star. Here in the Kingdom of Fantasy, you can have lots of adventures. You'll meet dragons and giants and terrifying sea serpents."

The Kingdom of Fantasy? I gulped. It sounded like a horribly scary place. Oh, how I missed my safe, cozy mouse hole. I took off my glasses so I could cry freely.

The Knight in Shining Armor rode fearlessly on his trusty white horse. His red cape flapped in the wind. His whiskers stood at attention. His sword clanged at his side.

Scribblehopper didn't notice.

But he did notice the music box in my backpack.

"Great jumping tadpoles!" he croaked. "That belongs to *Blossom*, Queen of the Fairies!"

In a flash, Scribblehopper had pulled the rose-colored scroll out of the music box. "This message is written in the FANTASIAN ALPHABET," he went on. Suddenly, his eyes bulged out. "Leaping lizards!" he cried. "Queen Blossom is in terrible danger. She says that only you can help her!"

I twirled my tail nervously. I wasn't a hero. I was just an ordinary mouse.

"I know it's hard to believe the Queen of the Fairies would call on *you*," Scribblehopper

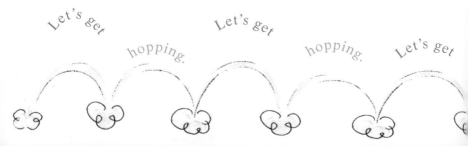

Let's get hopping. Let's get hopping. Let's get

This is the message from the Queen of the Fairies. To decipher the Queen's message, see the instructions on page 315.

Let's get hopping.

snorted. "I mean, look at that **pimple** on your snout. It's awful. But what Queen Blossom wants, Queen Blossom gets. We will have to cross six whole kingdoms to reach the Kingdom of the Fairies. So let's get hopping. Let's get jumping. Let's make like bees and buzz on out of here!"

I sighed. What could I do? As I said, I'm not a brave mouse, but I would never ignore a cry for help.

I took a deep breath. Then I raised my paw in the air. "I, *Geronimo Stilton*, promise to save the Queen of the Fairies!" I announced, trying to look tough. Too bad my knees felt as weak as cream cheese and I had a **pimple** on my snout.

I promise to save Queen Blossom!

32

THE KINGDOM OF THE WITCHES

Scribblehopper *grinned*. "Good move, Sir Geronimo of Stilton," he approved.

Scribblehopper told me we were about to enter the first kingdom. It was called the Kingdom of the Witches. It was always nighttime in the kingdom because the witches hated sunlight.

I gulped. Did I mention I'm afraid of the dark?

The kingdom was protected by **giant scorpions**.

I cringed. Did I mention I'm afraid of bugs?

 The witches had a bad habit of turning strangers into **piles of ashes**.

I began to sob uncontrollably. Did I mention I'm afraid of being burned to a crisp by a nasty witch?

Scribblehopper patted my shoulder. "Don't worry, Sir Geronimo," he croaked. "This kingdom will be easy for a **brave** knight like you. No sweat. No big deal. No problem-o."

I felt faint, but the frog didn't notice. He picked up his pen. "Any noble words to proclaim before entering the Kingdom of the Witches?" he asked.

By now, I was beside myself with fear. Oh, how did I get myself into this horrible mess?

"Yes, I have something to say," I whispered. "I'm scared!"

The frog ignored me. Instead, he began scribbling:

> *The Knight in Shining Armor boldly urged on his white horse, shouting, "Never fear, I'm on my way! Sir Geronimo of Stilton will save the day!"*

The Door to the Kingdom of the Witches

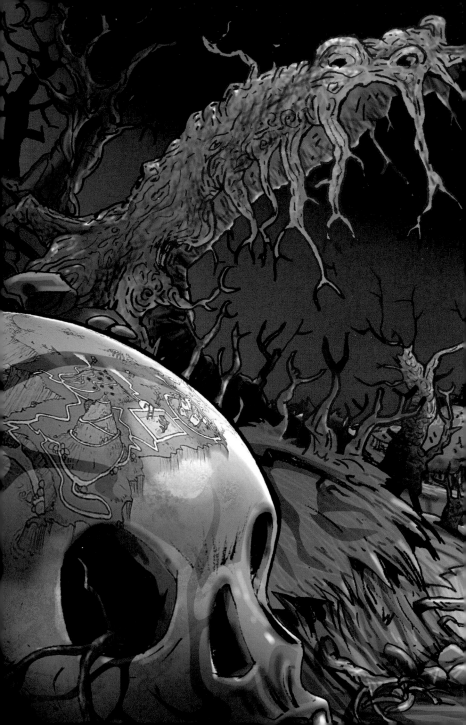

A NIGHTMARISH LAND

On shaky paws, I walked through the Ruby Door. At that moment, I heard a sound coming from the music box. It was a musical note: a **middle C** to be exact. How strange!

I pulled out the box from my pocket. The ruby had sprung open. Hidden beneath the ruby was a mysterious little plant. How odd!

Scribblehopper pointed to a map. A very scary map.

"This is the map of the Kingdom of the Witches!" he announced.

The names of the places made my fur crawl.

Brrrrrrrrrrrrrrrrrrrrrrrrrrrrrrrrrrrrrrrrrrrr!

The Kingdom of the Witches

Color: Red   **Gem:** Ruby   **Metal:** Bronze

Musical Note: Middle C

Queen: Cackle, Never-named, Queen of Darkness, Empress of Evil, Sorceress of Sorrow, Teacher of Terror, General of the Dark Army and All Things Unruly and Rotten

Royal Palace: Fortress of Fear, an extremely high tower made of skulls. It's the shape of a witch's hat. It is surrounded by a moat brimming with giant scorpions.

Guardian of the Kingdom: Arachne, a humongous spider with many legs. Also known as the Red-eyed Monster

Currency of the Kingdom: A bewitched golden coin

Spoken Language: Witchianese

History of Its Inhabitants: According to legend, witches dance in the woods on special nights such as Halloween (October 31). They vanish before the first crowing of the rooster. Those who pass through the Kingdom of the Witches must not drink or eat anything, or they'll never be able to leave again!

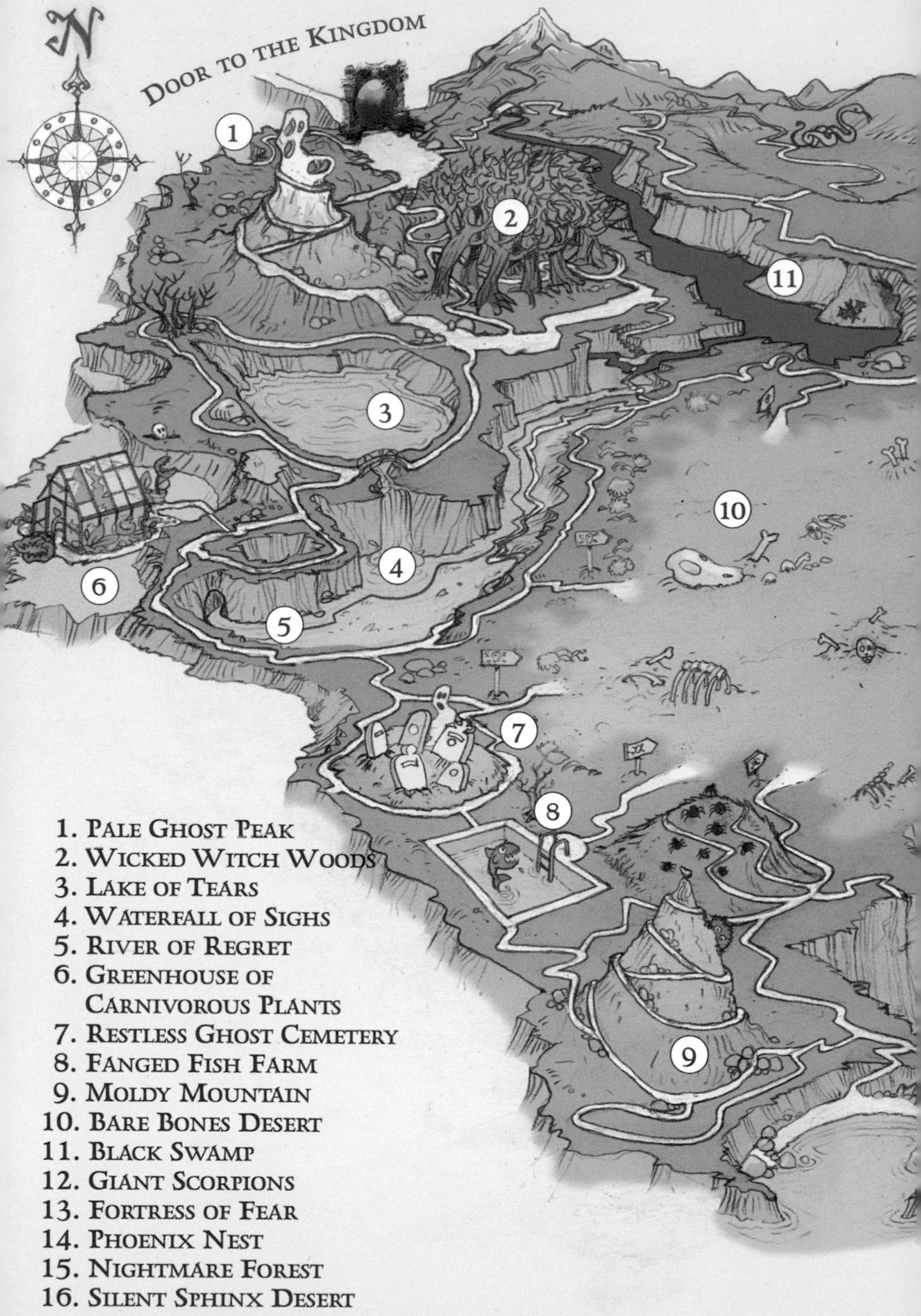

DOOR TO THE KINGDOM

1. PALE GHOST PEAK
2. WICKED WITCH WOODS
3. LAKE OF TEARS
4. WATERFALL OF SIGHS
5. RIVER OF REGRET
6. GREENHOUSE OF
   CARNIVOROUS PLANTS
7. RESTLESS GHOST CEMETERY
8. FANGED FISH FARM
9. MOLDY MOUNTAIN
10. BARE BONES DESERT
11. BLACK SWAMP
12. GIANT SCORPIONS
13. FORTRESS OF FEAR
14. PHOENIX NEST
15. NIGHTMARE FOREST
16. SILENT SPHINX DESERT

The Kingdom of the Witches

13

14

12

16

15

Land mile
Nautical mile
Fantasian mile

"**Black Swamp?** Moldy Mountain? Nightmare Forest? I want to go back! I want to go hoooooooooome! I want to go to the Ratlin's Tropical Resort and Health Spa and sip mozzarella milk shakes by the beach!" I sobbed.

"It's too late, Sir Geronimo," Scribblehopper said. "You should have thought of that before you stepped through that door. **NOW SHAKE A PAW!** You don't want to keep the Queen of the Fairies waiting!"

Then he pulled out his pen and wrote:

The Knight in Shining Armor looked over the map of the Kingdom of the Witches. Then he laughed. "This place looks like fun for a brave warrior like me!" he observed.

We made our way up Pale Ghost Peak. The wind **HOWLED** furiously in our ears.

OOOOOOOOOOOOOH!

Then we trampled through Wicked Witch Woods. Bare branches from the trees clawed at my fur. Next we crossed over the Lake of Tears, the Waterfall of Sighs, and the stinky River of Regret. **Rancid** rat hairs! This place was depressing.

After the river, we finally made it to the Restless Ghost Cemetery. Holey cheese, was I exhausted! I had to lean against a TOMBSTONE so I could catch my breath. I just hoped the ghost wouldn't find me.

KNIGHTS WITHOUT HEARTS

Suddenly, the ground began to shake beneath my paws. Cheese sticks! It was the restless ghost! I just knew it! The phantom was coming for me! I wondered what it'd been up to under those tombstones. Was it shooting the breeze with some skeletons? Playing dominoes with the undead? It was all too **GRUESOME** to picture. I closed my eyes. But when I opened them, there was no ghost rising up from the ground. Instead, I saw a band of knights on horseback, galloping right at us.

"It's the **HEARTLESS HORSEMEN**! Quick, hide!" Scribblehopper cried.

In a flash, we ducked behind two tombstones. "Who are the Heartless Horsemen?" I asked the frog. Two hours later, Scribblehopper finished his answer. Did I mention the frog likes to talk? He's a bigger **chatterbox** than my cousin Gabby Fur. She once talked the ear off a statue at the Mouseum of Modern Art. It took three tubes of superglue to get the ear back on.

Anyway, it seems these horsemen had been *good* knights at one time. **But then they turned terribly evil.** They became part of the **DARK ARMY**. They spread bad will and rotten feelings around the kingdom.

I shivered as the horsemen passed by. I was feeling pretty rotten myself. Oh, what miserable luck to be stuck in this terrifying **PLACE**!

THE RED-EYED MONSTER

Soon we found ourselves in the BARE BONES DESERT. Skeletons dotted the landscape as far as the eye could see.

"Come, Geronimo of Stilton!" Scribblehopper called. "It is time for you to face your first challenge."

I broke out in a cold sweat. First challenge? Wasn't this whole place challenging enough?

Scribblehopper didn't seem to notice that I was sweating like a sprinkler. He pointed out two sharp tusk-shapes rising out of a mound of **RED EARTH**. "Here you must battle Arachne, the RED-EYED MONSTER," he said.

My fur rose with fright. Thoughts raced through my mind. In ancient Greek, arachne (pronounced ah-RACK-knee) means "spider." Was the Red-eyed Monster a spider?

Before I could **SCREAM** "I want my mommy!" I found myself stuck in an invisible SPIDERWEB.

"**HELP!**" I screamed in horror.

Scribblehopper had been caught, too. He croaked with fright.

The red earth trembled. Eight massive hairy legs stretched out before us. Two enormous red eyes stared at me hypnotically. I couldn't move. I couldn't think. I couldn't breathe. An eensy-weensy spider could make my whiskers tremble. But this GIANT ONE had me paralyzed!

The Red-eyed Monster crawled toward me, creeping over the bones.

At last, I found my voice. "I am traveling to the Kingdom of the Fairies! I must save *Queen Blossom*!" I squeaked.

The spider rolled her large eyes. "Fairies? Who cares about fairies?" she **HISSED**. "Arachne only takes orders from the Queen of the Witches. And she tells Arachne to stop all strangers like you in the BARE BONES DESERT."

I could feel Scribblehopper shaking next to me. "Uh, Good Knight, I think if you told Arachne a story, she might like it," he suggested.

I nodded. "Would you like to hear a tale about your name, Arachne?" I tried.

The spider yawned. "Hurry up and tell it. But remember, Arachne doesn't like tricks," she warned.

I started to tell the tale.

THE MYTH OF ARACHNE
An ancient Greek legend

Long ago, many gods and goddesses lived on Mount Olympus. The goddess of wisdom and arts was named Athena.

At that time, there also lived a maiden called Arachne. She was a talented weaver.

"This girl has golden hands," people said.

"What an artist!" they proclaimed.

All this praise made Arachne proud, and soon she became boastful. "If I challenged the goddess Athena, I would be victorious!" she announced.

One day, the gossipy nymphs of the woods repeated Arachne's words to Athena. The goddess became angry. She challenged Arachne to a weaving contest.

The day of the contest, Athena wove with all her might, but when she finished, she realized that Arachne's work was better then hers. Angry at her defeat, the goddess ripped her rival's work into a thousand pieces!

Then she transformed the maiden into a spider.

And so, to this day, when you see a spider weaving its web, think of the fate of the maiden Arachne, the unhappy weaver turned into a hairy spider!

EVERYONE NEEDS FRIENDS!

I finished telling my tale.

Arachne stared at me. Her eyes grew huge. Suddenly, she began to shake. She began to sniff. She opened her jaws W I D E , baring her razor-sharp fangs.

Is this how it would all end? I'd become lunch meat for a monstrous spider?

But instead of eating, Arachne started crying. "**BOOOOOO-HOOOOOOOOOOO!**" she sobbed.

"Thank you for the story, my friend," the spider said. "I haven't cried like this since I was a baby spider just hatched

Arachne newly hatched from her egg!

from my egg! I am so bored and lonely here in the desert. There's nothing to do all day except devour passersby!"

I paled. But I felt sorry for her. Loneliness is a terrible thing. I mean, everyone needs friends, even giant spiders. And so I made a deal. "If you let us go, I will write down my story for you. That way you can read it over and over again. It will keep you company."

The spider cried tears of happiness.

I cried happily, too. I was going to live!

THE FORTRESS OF FEAR

We started walking again until we came to a fortress shaped like a witch's hat. According to the map, it had to be the **Fortress of Fear**. Swarms of vultures glided around, searching for bones they could pick dry.

I saw something shining white on the ground. I picked it up. It was a SKULL!

In a moat surrounding the fortress, giant scorpions waved their poisonous stingers. CLACK, CLACK, CLACK! I felt dizzy.

When I looked up, I felt even dizzier. "It'll be a tough climb to the top of the fortress," I said to Scribblehopper.

The frog roared with laughter. "Oh, Geronimo

of Stilton, you are so funny. You cannot climb to the top," he chuckled. "And even if you did, you'd never manage to get inside. The witches know how to defend themselves. They pour down cauldrons of **boiling oil** and heated tar and feathers. But I know a secret passageway. It was described to me by my grandmother Frogster, who was the cousin of the hairdresser of the nephew of the doorman of the sister of the podiatrist of the butler of the sister-in-law of the tailor of the fortune-teller of Never-named!"

"Never-named?" I asked. "Who's that?"

Again Scribblehopper roared with laughter. "Fair Knight, what planet are you from? Everyone knows who Never-named is." Then his voice dropped to a whisper. "Never-named is the QUEEN OF THE WITCHES," he explained. "She uses her **MAGIC POWERS** to bully others."

I was furious. No one should use their powers

to harm others. What an outrage! What a tragedy! What a witch!

Scribblehopper sighed. "Now I'll show you the secret passageway. But I want your *word of honor* that you'll never tell it to anyone," he insisted.

I held up my paw. "You have my rodent's *word of honor*,"* I said. And I meant it.

*I always keep my word. And so, I'm afraid that the Well of Fools with the entrance to the secret passageway isn't shown on the map of the Kingdom of the Witches. I'm sorry, dear readers, but a promise is a promise.

THE WELL OF FOOLS

Scribblehopper slid across the ground. "Slink like a salamander, just like me. That way, they won't spot us from the fortress," the frog advised. "Witches not only have magic powers, but they also have incredible eyesight. And they have amazing aim. I wouldn't want them throwing stuff down on us. They can hit an ant right between the eyes from a mile away."

We crept along toward the WELL OF FOOLS.

SLINKING LIKE A SALAMANDER!

Who knows how it had gotten that name?

The witches threw all sorts of things down at us:

- *a chipped pot*
- *a* **SMELLY** *old slipper*
- *a rotten cauliflower*
- *an old broomstick*

The pot clunked me on the snout. The slipper made me sneeze. The cauliflower dripped slimy mold all over my fur. And the broomstick nearly took off my tail. **Cheese niblets!** I'd need a long vacation if I made it home after this adventure.

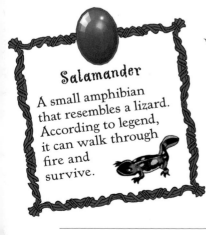

Salamander

A small amphibian that resembles a lizard. According to legend, it can walk through fire and survive.

At last, we reached the WELL OF FOOLS. We grabbed on to a small pail that was dangling from a rope. Slowly, we lowered ourselves down. Bony skeletons shone in the darkness at the bottom of the well. Now I knew why this place was called the Well of Fools. Only a fool would try to get into the fortress this way!

I was just about to die of fright when a gust of wind **BLEW THROUGH** my whiskers. Scribblehopper pointed to a hole in the wall of the well. It was **THE SECRET PASSAGEWAY**!

The passage led directly into the **Fortress of Fear**. We began climbing a very steep staircase. It was tough going. My heart was hammering. My fur was sweating. I was exhausted.

Finally, after a million hours, we reached a tiny trapdoor. I pushed it open carefully.

Secret passageway!

What did I see? I saw a whole mess of smelly feet. P.U.! I could barely breathe. We had wound up right in the middle of the fortress's **ballroom**. The smelly feet whirled and twirled around the room. The whole time, their owners—the witches—cackled in high-pitched voices. What an **ugly** sound!

Then things got even uglier. The witches had spotted us.

"**How did you get in here?**" one shrieked.

"**Who are you?**" another growled.

Some of them started to yank at my whiskers. Others pinched my tail.

"**Let's throw them to the vultures. They'd love a nice furry treat,**" one witch cackled. I turned as pale as a piece of mozzarella.

Scribblehopper didn't look much better. The

witches ripped at his clothes. "I want his hat! I want his vest!" they cried.

The plumpest of them all licked her lips.

"Let's take them to the kitchen. I could go for some roasted rodent with a side of frog flambé," she giggled.

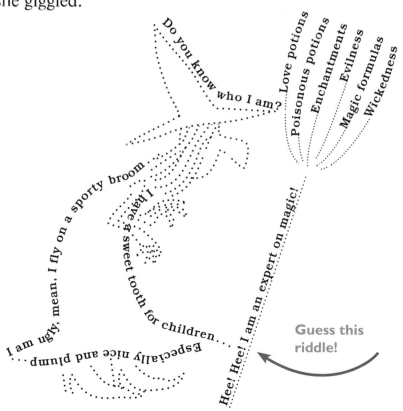

Do you know who I am?

Love potions
Poisonous potions
Enchantments
Evilness
Magic formulas
Wickedness

I fly on a sporty broom

I have a sweet tooth for children...

I am ugly, mean,

Especially nice and plump

Hee! Hee! I am an expert on magic!

Guess this riddle!

THE QUEEN OF THE WITCHES

Just then, a mysterious voice filled the room. "STOP, MY SISTERS!" it ordered. THEN THE VOICE COMMANDED US TO STEP FORWARD. UH-OH. SOMETHING TOLD ME THIS WAS NO ORDINARY WITCH. She sounded like the big cheese.

My paws shook with every step. BRRRRRRR! I felt like Dorothy when she's about to face the Wizard of Oz. The walls of the royal palace glimmered in the light. They were made of a thousand tiny white bones that had been polished to perfection. There were hundreds of **FLAMING TORCHES** and pots of burning incense. On one wall, I saw a thousand golden mirrors. I checked out my fur as I passed by.

What a disaster. I'd have to make an appointment at Clip Rat's Salon and Day Spa when I got home. Maybe I'd even try a new style.

My thoughts were interrupted by a wave of cackles. **Hee hee hee!**

Ha ha ha!

Ho ho ho!

On another wall, I spotted a thousand grinning mouths. I had a feeling the joke was on me. Oh, why had I ever sneaked into this **awful** place? I wondered if it was too late to get back into the well.

A shower of fleas rained down on my head. I looked up. A tiny bat hung from the rafters. It was picking the fleas from its wings. Rancid rat hairs! Did I mention I'm afraid of bugs?

I was about to grab my tail and run for the door

when I saw her. It was the Queen of the Witches. She had very fair skin and flaming red hair.  One of her eyes was **black** and the other was green. She sat on a throne made of prickly thorns. Two humongous crows* sat perched on either side of the throne. Scuttling around her was a swarm of cockroaches with tiny gold collars.

The Queen of the Witches leaned forward and looked us over.

"P-p-pleased to m-m-meet you, Your Majesty," stammered Scribblehopper.

Queen Never-named threw him an icy smile. Then she turned to me. "Who are you, stranger, and what

*Queen Never-named's two crows are called Shriek and Screech. Every morning, she sends them out to spy on her kingdom. At night, they return to tell her all of the secrets they've overheard.

do you want?" she cackled.

By now, I was feeling FAINT. I mean, the Queen of the Witches herself was sort of pretty. But who ever heard of a cockroach for a pet? And what was with the THORNY chair? Wasn't she uncomfortable?

I bowed before her. "Oh, Your Witchness, my name is . . ." I began.

JUST CALL ME CACKLE

But before I could finish, Scribblehopper broke in. "His name is Sir Geronimo of Stilton. He is a knight in **shining** armor!" he cried.

I shook my head. When would Scribblehopper learn? I wasn't a knight. I was just a plain old mouse. But there was no time to argue about it now.

"Oh, *Your Witchness*, I ask for your permission to cross through your kingdom," I blurted out.

"Call me Cackle," murmured the Queen of the Witches in a sweet voice. "Of course, you may cross. Now come **sit down** beside me."

I cringed. But what could I do? I wasn't about to argue with a witch. I sank down on a cushion of gray fur.

RATS! It felt strangely like mouse fur.

"Be careful," Scribblehopper whispered. "She's asked you to sit in on the *Great Council of Witches*. It's made up of the scariest witches from all over the world!"

I glanced around. The witches glared at me with penetrating stares. I shivered. There were no beauty contestants here. One had a mouthful of **iron teeth**. Another had **razor-sharp fingernails**. A third smelled like moldy cheese and another sported **greasy hair**. The witch closest to me had an ear full of hairy warts. I wondered if it was hard to hear with all those warts.

Suddenly, I saw a tiny speck in the sky.

"**Watch out, Geronimo of Stilton,**" Scribblehopper hissed. "That strange creature is called a **basilisk**. If you look it in the eyes, you'll be turned to stone!"

The basilisk gave Queen Cackle a letter. She read it and smiled. It was a list of all of the members of the **DARK ARMY**.

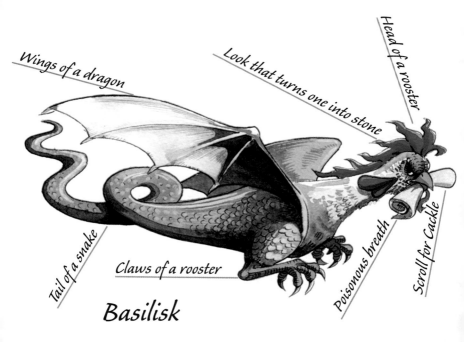

Wings of a dragon

Look that turns one into stone

Head of a rooster

Scroll for Cackle

Poisonous breath

Claws of a rooster

Tail of a snake

Basilisk

THE DARK ARMY OF CACKLE, THE QUEEN OF DARKNESS

I will obey my Queen!

10,000 HEARTLESS HORSEMEN. This gloomy league of empty armors is ruled by the will of Cackle, the Queen of Darkness.

I will tear you to pieces!

6,732 OGRES. These gigantic bodyguards wield spiked clubs and thick chains.

Graaack!

5,568 VST'S (VULTURES WITH STEEL TALONS) These are dangerous flying birds with deadly metallic talons.

3,798 PYGMY OGRES from Stinky Valley. They are small, smelly ogres that attack their victims with heavy lead bowling balls.

I am a small and smelly pest.

Slurp!

2,654 KILLER LICE. These are enormous lice as big as elephants, and they love to suck blood.

3,230 CHUBBY WRESTLERS. They squash their enemies by sitting on top of them while letting out a piercing scream: "Ayaaaa!"

Ayaaaa!

Ha! Ha! Ha!

2,123 MANIACAL TICKLERS. They tickle their enemies pitilessly until they surrender.

Screech! Screech! Screech! Screech!

1,000 GIANT BLACK SCORPIONS. They keep guard over the Fortress of Fear. They have sharp pincers and poisonous tails.

Clack!

1,947 SCREECHING JUMPING JACKS. They screech incessantly.

Ouhhhhhhh!

1,215 HOWLING HOWLERS. These creatures hide behind visitors and let out blood-curdling howls.

Now I'm going to make a stink!

976 STINKY MONSTERS from Moldy Mountain. These disgusting furry balls smell like moldy cheese.

Grrrrrrrrrrrr!

I am as hungry as a wolf!

875 COLOSSAL CHEWING MASTIFFS. These massive dogs have super-extra-enormous fangs.

695 WEREWOLVES. These monstrous creatures have fur as spiky as iron nails, pointy fangs, and razor-sharp claws.

Snic!

599 ARMORED BEETLES. Each one is as large as a three-story house and is covered with steel shells.

Attaaaack!

585 GIANT SOLDIER ANTS. They spray corrosive liquid and march in a squadron seven lines deep.

Burp!

Burp!

480 CARNIVOROUS FLOWERS. They imprison their enemies between their steel-like petals.

Splash!

240 DREAM-SUCKERS AND NIGHTMARE-MAKERS. These creatures rule the night.

Just a little joke!

Spuz!

99 POLTERGEISTS. These mischievous small ghosts perform tricks like making furniture and objects fly.

13 BLIND, SPITTING, SCHEMING PHANTOMS. These ghosts have bad breath and love to spit.

I thirst for blood!

Swisssssssh!

3 AUTHENTIC TRANSYLVANIAN VAMPIRES. They are related to Count Dracula.

2 FLYING STEEL FISTS. These gigantic mechanical flying hands move by the will of the Queen of the Witches.

Keep away from me!

1 GIGANTIC SPIDER. Her name is Arachne of the Bare Bones Desert.

SNAKES FOR HAIR AND SCORPIONS FOR JEWELS

While Queen Cackle was reading her letter, I looked around the room. I noticed a bronze cauldron next to the Queen of Darkness's chair. Inside it, a mysterious green potion bubbled and boiled. It had a pleasantly sweet smell, sort of like melted lollipops.

Just then, a snake slithered up to me. He was carrying a tray of yummy-looking desserts and drinks on his head. My mouth started to water. My tummy started to grumble. Cheese sticks, I was hungry! But just as I reached for a treat, Scribblehopper slapped my paw.

"Uh, no thanks, O Wonderful Queen," he mumbled. "Sir Geronimo is on a diet."

It was then that I remembered what the frog had told me about the Kingdom of the Witches. If you eat or drink anything while you're there, you'll be forced to stay forever!

"Don't be shy," Queen Cackle insisted. "Try a **honey** biscuit."

I shook my head.

"What do you say to some GOAT CHEESE?" she offered. "**Cookies**, candies, cakes?"

I declined.

"Well then, how about one teeny-tiny-eensy-weensy sip of WATER?" she pressed.

I could tell she was getting annoyed. But I had no choice. I didn't want to live in the Kingdom of the Witches. I was a mouse, after all. I belonged on Mouse

Island with my friends, my family, and Squeaker's All-U-Can-Eat Cheese Palace on Route 10. "No thank you." I squeaked in a small voice.

Suddenly, she flew into a rage. Her hair turned into a mass of **twisting snakes**. Her clothing became ragged, and her jewels became scuttling scorpions.

THE QUEEN OF DARKNESS POINTED HER PINKIE FINGER AT ME. A BOLT OF LIGHTNING SHOT OUT.

"How dare you refuse me!" she shrieked. "I'll turn you and this frog into cockroaches, like all the other *foolish* travelers!"

Just then, something strange happened. The mysterious plant I had found in the music box began to wriggle in my pocket. I pulled it out.

Queen Cackle's eyes grew wide. "How did you get that mandrake plant?" she asked. "It hasn't grown here for a thousand years. I need it for my **evil potions**!"

Ahhhhhh!

Mandrake (or Mandragora)

A plant with reddish berries that can be a cure or a poison, depending on the dose used. Legend has it that wizards use mandrake to prepare love potions. It is hard to harvest, because when it is ripped from the ground, it lets out a deafening scream!

I stared at the plant. Who would think something so cute could be so **DEADLY**?

Suddenly Scribblehopper

piped up. "We'll give you this plant if you let us leave the kingdom," he suggested.

WEREWOLVES!

The mandrake plant squealed with joy. It jumped up on Queen Cackle's hand and began to dance.

How strange. Maybe it had a thing for gruesome witches with snake hair.

Meanwhile, the Queen of Darkness laughed with delight. She couldn't take her eyes off the plant. "It's a deal," she grinned.

Then she turned to the little bat hanging over our heads. "Itchy!" she shrieked. Take them to the phoenix! And stop playing with your fleas!"

The bat looked **insulted**. He zipped off in a swarm of fleas, motioning for us to follow him.

At the roof of the fortress, a **RED-WINGED** bird waited. It sort of reminded me of a very funny-looking chicken, but Scribblehopper said it was called a phoenix. The bird

Phoenix

A mythical bird with golden red feathers and a harmonious voice. It lives for approximately five centuries.

winked at Scribblehopper. Did they know each other? I was about to ask when the phoenix told us to climb onto its back.

"Hold on tight, O Geronimo of Stilton!" Scribblehopper advised.

Before I could squeak, the phoenix spread out its wings and sped off. My whiskers flapped in the breeze. I watched as the ground grew smaller and smaller. Cheese sticks! We were up so high! I felt dizzy. Did I tell you I'm afraid of heights?

It was a good thing I was so tired. I fell asleep before I could have a panic attack.

I woke up a little before **MIDNIGHT**. That's when the phoenix decided to send us skydiving. Well, it wasn't the bird's fault. The saddle on its back snapped in two. Scribblehopper and I went down in a whirl of feathers. "Heeeeellllllppppp!!" I shrieked.

Luckily, we landed in the Mossy Forest. Have you ever lain down on a bed of moss? It is very comfy. I was just starting to relax when Scribblehopper cleared his throat.

"Ahem, Brave Knight, there's one little problem with this forest," he murmured sadly. "You see, it's sort of full of **WEREWOLVES**."

Sort of full? How about all the way full! We were surrounded by a pack of **WEREWOLVES**! Their rotten fangs were **DRIPPING** with disgusting drool. Hadn't they ever heard of toothbrushes? Still, I wasn't about to give them any advice on oral hygiene. I had a feeling they wouldn't take it the right way.

Scribblehopper took off in a blur of green. I followed close behind. There was no way I was going to become **wolf chow**.

We headed toward a large yellow glittering stone, and ... *we passed through the Topaz Door!*

Werewolves

Men who change into wolves on the night of the full moon. While they howl at the moon, their claws emerge and thick fur begins to grow on their bodies.

The Door to the Kingdom
of the Mermaids

The beautiful sea!

AN ENCHANTED LAGOON WITH DEEP BLUE WATER

At that moment, the topaz in the music box slid open. I heard a strange musical note: a  *D*. Beneath the topaz was a **GOLDEN HAIRCOMB** decorated with more yellow gems.

Suddenly, I heard a splash. We were standing beside a lagoon. Deep blue waves glittered in

the sunlight. On the horizon I spotted a ship. I wondered if there were pirates on board.

I **CLIMBED** up a palm tree to get a better view, but the ship had already disappeared. Oh, well. One thing that didn't disappear was the fruit. It was all over the place. We **stuffed** our faces.

The whole time Scribblehopper rambled on and on. I guess his mother never told him that it's rude to **CROAK** with your mouth full.

CONKED OUT
BY A COCONUT

The Sea

Around three billion years ago, life was born from the sea. Its continuous moving waters are a symbol of birth and rebirth. However, the sea also has a dark side: It is terrifying when its waters are agitated by storms. And legends tell of monsters that emerge from its deepest depths.

After we ate, Scribblehopper lay down beneath a palm tree. "I think I ate too many bananas," he chuckled. He rubbed his tummy, then let out a noisy **burp**.

I plopped down beside him. "At last, a quiet, relaxing spot," I said with a sigh. "No spiders, no werewolves, no witches." I closed my eyes, feeling content. "What could go wrong here? Well, I guess I could get too much **sun**," I mused. "Or I could get too much sand. Or I could get hit on the head with a coconut."

Just then, A COCONUT HIT ME ON THE HEAD. I fainted.

Two seconds later, I came to. Scribblehopper was splashing cold water on my snout. "I'm awake, I'm awake," I spluttered.

The frog snickered. "Fair Knight, you are so FOOLISH. Why don't you put on your helmet?" he croaked.

I groaned. This knight thing was starting to get on my nerves. "I *don't have* a helmet because I'm *not* a knight!" I squeaked.

Scribblehopper wasn't listening. He was staring at a seashell. There was a map of the Kingdom of the Mermaids drawn on the shell. Now where did that come from?

"Follow me to the bottom of the sea, Good Knight," the frog said. "It's as easy as hopping."

I chewed my whiskers. I wasn't much of a hopper. As a mouse, I preferred to scamper.

The frog led me to a coral staircase rising up just above the waves. THEN HE STARTED HOPPING DOWN THE STEPS.

The Kingdom of the Mermaids

Color: Orange   **Gem:** Topaz   **Metal:** Silver

Musical Note: D

Queen: Her Marine Majesty Aquafin, Empress of the Great Blue, Queen of the Golden Sea, Princess of the Silver Fins, Lady of the Mermaids, Governor of the Grand Flippers, and Ruler of the World Under the Waves

Royal Palace: Coral Castle

Guardian of the Kingdom: The sea serpent

Currency of the Kingdom: Pearls

Spoken Language: Sirenese

History of Its Inhabitants: In Greek mythology, the sirens were daughters of the river god Achelous, who had the torso of a man and the legs of a bull. They fascinated sailors with their songs, luring them to the rocks and causing shipwrecks. In *The Odyssey* (a poem by Homer, written in the eighth century BCE), the cunning hero Odysseus heard their song. As a precautionary measure, he had his friends fill their ears with wax, and they tied him to his ship's mast so that he could enjoy their song.

DOOR TO THE KINGDOM

The Kingdom of the Mermaids

1. CORAL STAIRCASE
2. BLACKBEARD'S SHIP
3. DROWNED MAN WHIRLPOOL
4. GIANT MEDUSA
5. BLACK SHARK
6. NEPTUNE'S PIT
7. GIANT SQUID PIT
8. GRAND BUBBLE
9. ALGAE FOREST
10. ABYSS OF THE WHITE WHALES
11. COLOSSAL CRAB OF THE GREAT BLUE

12. PINK PEARL PEAK
13. CORAL CASTLE
14. SEA SERPENT
15. MORAY EEL'S DEN
16. ISLAND OF THE SEA LIONS
17. LIZARD LAGOON

THERE'S A SEA SERPENT BEHIND YOU!

I scampered behind Scribblehopper. "B-b-but I can't breathe underwater," I stammered.

He grinned. "This is a special sea," he said. "It's called the **Great Blue**. Try putting your head under the water."

Reluctantly, I stuck my snout beneath the waves. Cheesecake! I could breathe! And I could hear the voices of the fish!

I went down one step at a time, clutching the coral banister. Scribblehopper, on the other paw, was having a blast. He joked with the clownfish, chatted with the dolphins, and tickled the starfish.

Meanwhile, I was scared **out of my wits**. Everything looked spooky underwater. And what was that huge, dark shadow overhead? Rats! It was a killer whale!

The frog stopped his chatting. "LOOK OUT FOR THAT FISH!" he warned.

As we hid, I thought I would give Scribblehopper a quick science lesson. "The killer whale isn't a fish. It's a mammal, just like a dolphin," I explained.

After the killer whale swam away, I found myself snout-to-snout with a huge fish. It was a **GIANT SHARK**! Its eyes stared at me menacingly. My heart pounded under my fur. *I was so scared* I started sweating . . . underwater!

The shark looked me over like a piece of lunch meat. Or was it dinner? "Hmm, I've never tasted a rodent, but there's a first time for everything," it snarled.

I dived behind a reef.

"Come back here, mousey!" it *shrieked*, racing after me. Minutes later, it banged its head into the reef. "Waah! I want my mommy!" it cried. Then it swam off. And I thought I was a scaredy mouse!

Don't be silly!

We made our way farther down the coral steps. It was getting **DARKER** and **SPOOKIER**. I shivered. Even Scribblehopper had stopped chattering. Then he stopped hopping. "Look out, there's a **sea serpent** behind you!" he cried.

Yikes!

I rolled my eyes. "Oh, don't be silly," I scoffed. "**Sea serpents** don't exist."

The frog's eyes grew huge. "**N-n-no, really**," he

stammered. "There r-r-r-eally is a SEA SS-S-SERPENT behind you!"

I snorted. This frog must have thought I was born yesterday. I turned around just to show him I wasn't afraid. And I came snout-to-muzzle with a scaly, slimy, monstrous SEA SERPENT!

As I stared in horror, its jaws opened WIDE. I gulped. That sea serpent had more teeth than my great-uncle Chompers. Do you know him? He can chomp through a whole block of cheddar in one bite!

Heeeeeelp!

You're Sleepy, You're Veeery Sleeeepy...

The sea serpent's forked tongue **FLICKED IN AND OUT**. *Maybe he's just saying hello,* I told myself. I was trying to be brave.

"Uh, well, hello to you, too," I squeaked. "Seen any good movies lately?"

The serpent ignored me. It began to swim around me faster and faster. Its eyes drilled into mine. My head began to spin ...and spin and spin...

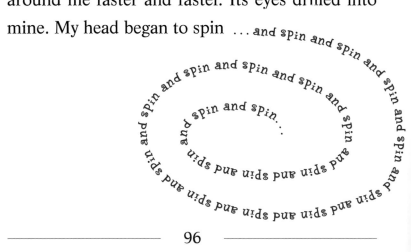

"You're getting sleepy, veeery sleeeepy..."

the serpent murmured.

Dazed, I realized that I really *was* sleepy. The sea serpent had coiled itself around us and was dragging us down to the

BOTTOM OF THE SEA!

A ROSE-COLORED CORAL CASTLE

I woke up in front of a majestic castle made of rose-colored coral surrounded by colorful algae. Scribblehopper told me this was Coral Castle. A troop of sea horses led by a merman escorted us to a long hall. At the end of the hall were two thrones made of pearl.

Both thrones were empty. On the dance floor a snobby-looking tuna wearing a tuxedo whirled around. He seemed to be giving *dancing lessons* to a mermaid with eyes the color of the sea. Her hair shimmered like the sun at sunset. The scales of her long tail were sparkly silver. She was Aquafin, the Queen of the Mermaids.

I watched as she **twirled** around faster and faster. She was making me dizzier than the sea serpent. Finally, she twirled right over to her throne and plopped down into it. A crab raced over with a tray of **pastries**. The "treats" looked worse than my grouchy grandma Onewhisker's **disgusting** spinach-and-cheese canapés.

> **Mermen**
>
> Male marine beings covered with scales, with the tails of fish and arms of humans. The mermen ride on carriages pulled by dolphins. Their tails can change to human legs so the mermen can walk on land.

A court of octopuses, crabs, oysters, and clams surrounded Aquafin, all chatting away. One baby **octopus** pointed at me and grinned. "I bet Her Majesty would like to take a bite out of that knight," it said with a smirk.

Its mother patted its tentacle. "My little **darling** is so observant," she boasted to

the other mothers in the crowd.

I twisted my tail up in knots. I was starting to get a really **BAD** feeling about this. I was feeling like I wanted to swim for my life!

Just then, I had an idea. I reached into my pocket and pulled out the **golden** haircomb. It wasn't long before Queen Aquafin noticed it. Within seconds, she had jumped off her throne, swum across the room, and yanked it out of my paw. Whatever happened to please and *thank you*?

"What is this?" she cried. "Oh, it's **adorable**! What beautiful sparkling jewels. I *loooooove* jewels!" She stuck the comb in her hair, then admired herself in her clamshell mirror.

Queen Aquafin

QUEEN AQUAFIN

The entire court showered her with compliments.

"It's *beautiful*, Your Majesty!" gushed a seahorse.

"It's so you!" agreed an octopus.

"Simply ssssstunning!" said a smiling shark.

Queen Aquafin silenced them with a THUMP of her tail. Then she shot me a coy smile. "Why, Knight, this is a perfectly adorable gift!" she purred.

I bowed my head. "Um, well, glad you like it. I was actually wondering if you could grant us permission to travel through your realm to the Kingdom of the Dragons," I said.

Queen Aquafin looked me over from head to tail. Then she slapped her hand on the empty throne beside her. "You're too adorable to leave

right away. Sit down here!" she commanded.

I bowed again. "I am honored by your offer, but I really need to be going," I squeaked.

Queen Aquafin shot me a look. "You don't think you can swim away just like that, do you? I'll be the one to tell you when you can leave. Now tell me an **adorable** story or I'll feed you to the **CARNIVOROUS CLAMS!**" she ordered.

I chewed my whiskers. "How about a **FAIRY TALE**?" I offered.

Queen Aquafin clapped her hands in delight. "Just make sure it's adorable!" she warned. "Or those clams will be munching tonight!"

I swallowed and began to tell the story.

When I finished, Queen Aquafin squealed with joy. "**Oh, what an adorable story!**" she cried. "**LISTEN UP, CREATURES!** I've decided this mouse is too adorable to let go. I'm going to marry

THE LITTLE MERMAID
By Hans Christian Andersen

Once upon a time, there was a little mermaid with the sweetest voice. She lived with her sisters at the bottom of the sea.

One day, during a bad storm, the little mermaid saw a handsome prince about to drown among the waves. She saved him and brought the unconscious prince to the beach. She had fallen deeply in love with him. But, of course, being a mermaid, she could never live on land. In desperation, she went to the wicked Sea Witch, who made this proposition:

"I will transform your fishtail into a pair of legs, so you can walk on dry land and look for the one you love. But, in exchange, you will have to give me your voice. If the prince does not marry you within a year, you will disappear and become the sea foam!"

The little mermaid was deeply in love with the prince, so she accepted the proposal. With her new legs, she ran to the prince's castle. Because she had no voice, she could not tell him that she was the one who had saved him.

A year went by, and the little mermaid grew more and more unhappy. She was about to lose every hope when her sisters came to her aid. They had cut their beautiful, long, golden hair and had given it to the Sea Witch in return for the lost voice of the little mermaid. The maiden, who could now speak, explained to the prince what had happened. Grateful and in love, he married her and the two lived happily ever after!

him and keep him here with me forever! Now I must have the most adorable wedding. I want a **bouquet** of sea anemones, a gown studded with pearls, a **DAZZLING** crown, and a wedding carriage drawn by a thousand SNOW-WHITE dolphins . . .

. . . a gown studded with pearls . . .

A bouquet of sea anemones . .

. . . a dazzling crown . . .

. . . and a wedding carriage drawn by a thousand snow-white dolphins . . .

...and I want it all by tomorrow!"

A tiny lobster tried to protest. "But, Your Majesty, we cannot do it all by tomorrow."

Queen Aquafin **swished** her tail with irritation. "Just do what I said!" she roared.

While the sea creatures were arguing, Scribblehopper and I made a mad dash for the coral stairs. But the Queen of the Mermaids noticed right away. "Come back here, or I'll turn you into **fish stew**!" she shrieked.

A CHORUS OF A THOUSAND MERMAIDS

Queen Aquafin grabbed a telephone made from a seashell. "Hello? **Blackbeard the Pirate?** A mouse and a frog are escaping. Stop them immediately! Especially the rodent!" she commanded.

The mermen blew their horns.

TOOT TOOT **TOOT TOOT-TOOT**

Then Queen Aquafin began to sing. A chorus of a thousand mermaids joined in. **Cheese niblets!** They were singing the "Song of the Sirens." It's a song with hypnotic powers. No one can resist it.

I need to go . . .
Queen Aquafin is calling . . .

"The sea is deep, the sea is wide
The sea is always on your side,
Listen to my voice
And you won't have a choice
Forever you'll remain
here with me with me with me . . ."

Nooooooooooo!

My head started to swim. My paws started to tremble. I was being hypnotized . . . again! Then I had an idea. Quickly, I tore off the hem of my jacket. I used it to plug up my ears. Then I gave some material to Scribblehopper.

My trick worked! We started **CLIMBING** up the stairs again. Then, just before we reached the surface, I **tripped**. The music box slipped from my backpack. It tumbled down into the sea.

I crawled onto the beach, sobbing. "Oh, how could I be such a **cheesehead**?" I cried. "I can't believe I lost Queen Blossom's music box!"

Just as I was about to tear out all of my fur, a **SEA TURTLE** rose

Sigh!

up from the bottom of the sea. It was carrying the music box in its mouth. It laid the box down on the sand beside me.

"My name is Shelly," she said. "I saw you drop Queen Blossom's music box and I thought you might need it."

WHAT LUCK! I was on cloud nine.

Then Shelly turned around. "Oh, one other thing. You'd better hurry. *Blackbeard*'s pirate ship is coming after you," she added.

My heart sank.

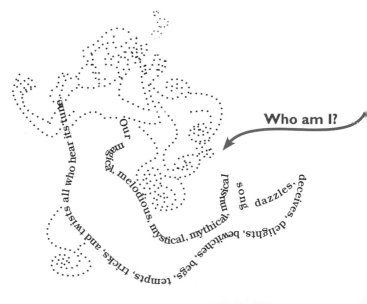

Who am I?

Our magical, melodious, mystical, mythical, musical song dazzles, deceives, delights, bewitches, begs, tempts, tricks, and twists all who hear its tune.

BLACKBEARD'S SHIP

"We're heading toward the Kingdom of the Fairies to save Queen Blossom, who's in trouble," I explained to Shelly.

The turtle nodded. "May I come with you?" she asked shyly.

I shook her paw. "We would be *honored*," I said.

This made Scribblehopper super-excited. "Now there will be three of us. We can be a team. We should make a name for ourselves. How about the Three Mouseketeers?" he suggested.

"**NO**. We're not all mice," I said. "How about the Dream Team?"

"**NO**. That's too sappy," said Scribblehopper.

"What about the Order of the Fairy Queen?!" offered Shelly.

We shook in agreement. "Long live the Order of the Fairy Queen!"

But just then, an **icy** wind made my whiskers quiver. Queen Aquafin had stirred up a **hurricane** to destroy us! The high winds whisked sand and palm trees from the island into the sky. They **tossed** us around like wet socks in a clothes dryer.

How much time passed? Seconds? Hours? Finally, the whirlwind died down and we found ourselves back on the beach. Shelly had cut herself on a sharp **reef**. I ripped off a strip of cloth from my shirt and bandaged up the wound. It wasn't an easy thing to do. You see, the sight of blood makes me feel faint!

Just as we were breathing a sigh of relief, a ship appeared on the horizon. Rats! **Blackbeard**'s ship was sailing right for us!

Shelly told us to climb onto her back. She swam toward the **Citrine Door**. It would lead us to the Kingdom of the Dragons.

The **turtle** stopped at the door. "I must leave you now," she said. "My injury will only slow you down. Thanks for letting me be a part of the team."

I felt **awful**. Shelly would never have been

hurt if she hadn't tried to help us. "Don't go," Scribblehopper and I cried.

But Shelly just smiled.

"It's OK," she said. "Don't be sad.

Remember, the hearts of friends will always be together."

The turtle pointed to a large yellow stone hidden in the palm trees.

"There's the Citrine Door that will take you to the Kingdom of the Dragons," she said.

It was midnight. We had to **HURRY**.

Waving good-bye to Shelly,

we walked through the Citrine Door!

The Door to the Kingdom
of the Dragons

THE RIVER OF FIERY LAVA

As we entered the Kingdom of the Dragons, the music box tinkled. I heard a musical note: an $\mathcal{E}$.

The citrine slid open. Out popped a gold tooth! It looked like it belonged to some giant creature. Cheese sticks! I wouldn't want to see the rest of those chompers.

I looked around. We were in the middle of a dry, SUN-BAKED wasteland. Steaming volcanoes stood on either side of us.

The sky was dimmed by a **dark cloud** of soot. Every once in a while, the ground **trembled**. Were the volcanoes about to blow? Was this how it would all end? I could

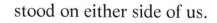

The Kingdom of the Dragons

Color: Yellow **Gem:** Citrine **Metal:** Gold

Musical Note: E

King: His Magnificent Majesty, King Firebreath III of Sizzling Cinder, of the noble dynasty of Smoldering Lava, King of Dragonaire, Emperor of the Volcano of Vapors, Count of the Steaming Sand Dunes, and Governor of all Great and Glowing Fireballs

Royal Palace: Dragonaire

Guardian of the Kingdom: Mount Thunder

Currency of the Kingdom: Dragonet doubloons

Spoken Language: Dragonese

History of Its Inhabitants: Dragons are two-footed or four-footed reptiles. They often have wings and spew out fire with each breath. Many dragons are the guardians of treasures. Dragons have extremely sharp vision. Some never sleep. In Greek, the word *dragon* means "serpent." Some famous dragons include: Ladon, who had one hundred heads and was the guardian of the Garden of Hesperides, where golden apples grew; Fafnir, who was slain by the German hero Siegfried; and the Chinese red dragon, Chien Tang, who was 1,000 feet long!

Door to the Kingdom

The Kingdom of the Dragons

just read the headlines now: Publisher
Buried Alive under Hot Lava!
Melted Mouse Mess Discovered in
Dragon Land!

My heart hammered under my fur. I was so nervous I didn't even notice we were sitting on an **enormouse** dragon's egg. A map of the Kingdom of the Dragons was drawn on it!

As usual, Scribblehopper started chattering away. He loved gossip. "Want to hear some dirt?" he asked.

What could I say? When he had something to say, there was no stopping Scribblehopper.

He told me that the King of the Dragons, Firebreath III, had a crush on *Princess Ashley*. But for some reason, he couldn't tell her.

Before I could ask why, we arrived at the River of Fiery Lava. A long, wobbly rope bridge dangled over it. Rats!

"I can't cross over that!" I sobbed. "I'm afraid of heights!"

Scribblehopper patted my back. "Don't be **silly**," he said. "So you might trip. So you might slip. So you might fall into a pit of scorching hot lava and boil up in seconds. You have to save Blossom, the Queen of the Fairies, remember?"

Oh, how I wished I could forget. I wished I could go home to my **cozy** mouse hole. Home to my megahuge fridge. Home to the electric cheese slicer I bought on sale at the Cheddar Chopper.

Instead, I put one **trembling** paw onto the bridge. "You can do it, Geronimo," I told myself. "Come on, be a mouse."

My head was spinning.

"Don't look down!" Scribblehopper warned. "And remember to take it one hop at a time. That's what my grandmother WARTY always told me."

I took one *tiny* step out onto the bridge. A few more steps and I would be safe. But then disaster struck. A splotch of lava shot up and set fire to the bridge! "**HELP! HELP!**" I shrieked in horror.

In a flash, Scribblehopper grabbed my paw. We bounced to the other side of the bridge just as it crumbled.

Scribblehopper began to *scribble* away. . . .

> *The Knight in Shining Armor leaped onto the bridge. He wasn't afraid.*
> *He was the bravest knight ever!*

I was touched. "Thank you, Scribblehopper," I squeaked. "You are a **TRUE FRIEND**."

Now if I could just get him to eat cheese instead of flies!

Grandma always says, "Take everything one hop at a time!"

Grandma Warty
Scribblehopper's grandmother loved to paint and give advice.

THE SECRET OF MOUNT THUNDER

We trudged along **LAVA LAKE** and the flaming **SPRING OF FIRE**. Holey cheese! It was hot!

We crept around **DRAGON CEMETERY**. It was full of dragon skeletons. I was scared out of my wits!

Finally, we arrived at **MOUNT THUNDER**. It was an enormous mountain made up of thousands of stones balanced on top of one another.

"There are lots of stories about Mount Thunder," Scribblehopper explained. "But no one knows its secrets because no one ever lives to tell about it!"

I stared at the tottering mountain. Not a single plant grew on it. **HOW STRANGE!**

Just then, a bird landed on one of the stones. It pecked at it, searching for a worm. A dozen stones tumbled downward.

The mountain **trembled**.

That's when I had a terrifying thought. Even the slightest noise could cause an avalanche!

Now I knew what we had to do to get to the other side of Mount Thunder. We had to be **QUIET**.

Of course, I knew I could keep my snout shut. After all, I learned how to be quiet as a mouse in grade school. But what about that **CHATTERBOX** Scribblehopper? I glanced at my new friend. This might be his hardest challenge yet.

Quickly, I picked up a stone and wrote down a message. It said, **SILENCE**!

Scribblehopper opened his mouth, but I held up my paw. I pointed to my message.

We began climbing Mount Thunder. It was tough going. But soon we got to the top. We climbed down the other side in total silence. I was so excited, I wanted to squeak. I wanted to squeal. I wanted to kick up my paws and do a jig. We were doing it! We were conquering Mount Thunder!

Then, just before we reached the bottom, Scribblehopper sneezed.

I felt the ground tremble. I heard a thundering noise. **Bam! Boom! Bam!**

A tremendous avalanche came crashing down Mount Thunder. We ran. Lucky for us, the stones never caught up with us. We were safe!

DRAGONAIRE

Scribblehopper and I sat down to rest. I was beat. I closed my eyes. I pictured myself soaking in a warm, *bubbly*, cheese-scented bathtub. No lava-spouting volcanoes. Just me. The bubbles. And a sharp stick in my side?

My eyes popped open. A huge green, scaly dragon with **red eyes** stood in front of me. It was poking me with a long, sharp spear.

It was Ember, Captain of the Dragon Guards. "Who are you? And how did you get over Mount Thunder?" he roared. His fiery breath nearly took off my *whiskers*. I wondered if he'd ever tried breath mints.

"My name is *Stilton* . . ." I began.

He cut me off. "Follow me to the royal palace!" he commanded.

By the time we arrived at the palace, the sun was setting. What a sight! The palace was a tall volcano that belched out gray smoke.

So this was

DRAGONAIRE!

The sky was thick with flying dragons taking off and landing. It was just like being at an airport. The dragons took turns taking off from a **RUNWAY** right below us.

One dragon stood in the control tower with a megaphone. It seemed to be directing traffic. **"Left! Right! Hey, watch your tail!** Can't you see there's another dragon taking off before you? Wait your turn, Burn Brain!"

We walked through a large doorway.

"Halt! Who goes there?" a voice called out.

"It's the Captain of the Dragon Guards," Ember announced. "I need to see King Firebreath!"

Ember led us down a long hallway. The walls were painted with scenes of dragon battles.

At last, we reached a large room. It was lit by a chandelier made up of flaming candles. Fiery lava gushed up from a stone fountain in the center of the room. A plump little dragon beat on a gong to announce our entrance.

BOOOOONNNGGGGGGGGGGGGG!

FIREBREATH III OF SIZZLING CINDER

As soon as the gong sounded, all of the dragons in the room stopped talking. I noticed they were all seated around a **LONG** stone table. It looked like they were about to eat dinner. I shivered. I hoped mouse wasn't on the menu.

Just then, the **King of the Dragons** stood up. His muscular body was covered with glistening

green scales. He had wings that looked like they'd been sprinkled with a golden powder. On his ankle was a tattoo. It was a picture of a lady dragon and the letter *A*. Could it be *Princess Ashley*?

The king let out a loud snort. "Who is it? Who's bothering me?" he growled.

The royal butler cleared his throat. Then he began to recite all of the king's titles in a high, whiny voice. "Let me introduce . . .

His Magnificent Majesty, King Firebreath III
of Sizzling Cinder,
of the noble dynasty of
Smoldering Lava, King of Dragonaire,
Emperor of the Volcano of Vapors,
Count of the Steaming Sand Dunes,
and Governor of All Great
and Glowing Fireballs!"

As the butler spoke, fire shot from his mouth. Suddenly, he accidentally breathed on his own tail. It quickly caught on **FIRE**. He ran around squealing. Another dragon raced after him, trying to put out the butler's tail.

It was a funny sight. Scribblehopper and I snickered softly.

"Who's laughing?" King Firebreath shouted. "*I'm* not laughing, so no one else should be laughing. Is that clear?"

Ember bowed before the King of the Dragons. "These two **STRANGERS** survived Mount Thunder," he said. "I brought them here as a gift for His Majesty."

The entire court clapped. "Roasted rodent and frog flambé? Yum! Yum!" they cheered.

King Firebreath **STARED** off into space. He didn't seem to be listening. I also wondered why he kept covering his mouth whenever he spoke. Did he have bad breath? Did he spit when he spoke?

It WAs ALL OnE BIg MYstERY.

Roasted Rodent

Frog Flambé

SUMMON THE ROYAL DENTIST!

I had to figure out King Firebreath's secret. So I came up with a plan. I started squeaking and running around in circles. The King of the Dragons was so startled his jaw dropped open in surprise. Then I understood his secret. He was missing a tooth.

Now I had another brilliant idea. I presented him with the golden tooth I'd found in the music box. "Here is a gift for you, Your Majesty," I said.

King Firebreath picked up the tooth. He tried it on. "Why, it's perfect! It's as if it was made just for me!" he exclaimed. "Quick! Summon the royal dentist!"

A **BRIGHT GREEN** dragon skittered in.

The King of the Dragons pointed to his new tooth. "See how it's done?!" he shouted. "For years, I've been asking you to figure out a way to fix my smile. But you insisted that it was impossible!"

The dentist turned a **PALE APPLE-GREEN** color.

"I should throw you into **LAVA LAKE** for this!" King Firebreath went on.

The dentist turned a sickly looking **DROOL GREEN**.

"Lucky for you I'm in a good mood today," the King of the Dragons continued. "Now that I've got my charming grin back, I can ask for my sweet

1. Happy　　2. Worried　　3. Terrified　　4. About to faint!

Ashley's hand in marriage. And, you will cancel my last ten years of dentist's bills!"

At that, the little dentist turned PUKE GREEN, slumped over, and fainted.

King Firebreath snorted. Then he ordered the royal cook to bring him a hundred pounds of caramel, five hundred boxes of taffy, and three tons of bubble gum. "The chewier the better!" he giggled. Next he demanded that the royal jester tell him **A JOKE**.

"But, Your Majesty, it's been thirty years since I've told a joke," the jester whined. "I don't think I can remember any."

The King of the Dragons rolled his eyes. He pointed a scaly claw at me. "You!" he demanded. "Tell me a joke! And make it a funny one!"

Terrified, I told him a joke.

What really bothers a dragon?

Having an inflamed throat!

THE FIRE BRAND

The joke wasn't even that funny, but the King of the Dragons doubled over in laughter. "Ha! Ha! Hee! Hee! Ho! Ho!" he shouted.

Next he called for his royal poet. "Write a *love letter* to Princess Ashley," King Firebreath ordered. "Tell her that I want to marry her. And make it sappy. I want her to weep tears of joy. After all, I am quite a catch."

The royal poet ran off. "Don't worry, Your Fiery Highness," he called. "The letter will be so sweet, it will sizzle with your love!"

Just then the King of the Dragons remembered I was still in front of him. "Oh, I almost forgot about you, Furry Rodent," he chuckled. "Now make a wish and I will give you whatever you desire!"

I thanked King Firebreath for his generous offer and told him I really wanted to cross over to the next kingdom: the Kingdom of the Pixies.

"Do you really want to see the pixies? They're so annoying," the King of the Dragons said. Still, he agreed to grant my wish. "But first, I'll give you a pass that will allow you a safe journey," he explained.

He pressed his claw down against my paw. I heard a hissing noise. The air was filled with the smell of burned fur. Cheese niblets! Old Firebreath had just set fire to my paw!

I was about to run squeaking from the room when Scribblehopper stopped me. "The fire brand is the highest honor ever granted by the King of the Dragons," he told me. "It will prove that you are traveling with the permission of King Firebreath."

THE FIRE BRAND

I looked down at my paw. It now bore a brand in the shape of a **griffin**, which is a mythical monster with the head and wings of an eagle and the body and tail of a lion.

I choked out a "thank you" to King Firebreath. I would have shaken his claw, but my paw was still **smoking**!

STORIES ABOUT DRAGONS

We were just about to leave when King Firebreath called us back.

"**WAIT!** I love stories about dragons. If you know one, I'll give you a guide so you'll reach the border of my kingdom faster," he offered.

"Go on! Tell him a story!" I urged Scribblehopper.

He shook his head. "I don't know anything about dragons," he said. "You tell him one, Fair Knight."

I started to protest when the King of the Dragons began to growl. Fire shot from his mouth. "Oh, **sizzling** sand traps!" he shrieked. "Are you going to tell me a story or not?"

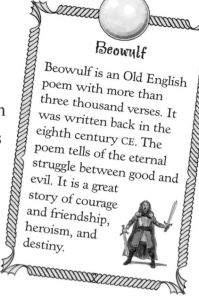

Beowulf

Beowulf is an Old English poem with more than three thousand verses. It was written back in the eighth century CE. The poem tells of the eternal struggle between good and evil. It is a great story of courage and friendship, heroism, and destiny.

Scribblehopper pushed me forward. "Sir Geronimo knows a splendid story about dragons, Your Royal Fire Starter," he lied.

I was ready to kill him. That frog was trying to get me fried! But suddenly, I remembered the story of **BEOWULF**.

I began to tell the tale.

BEOWULF
An Old English Poem

There once lived in a lake in Denmark a monster called Grendel. Every night, Grendel attacked the royal palace of Hrothgar, the King of the Danes, and devoured his subjects!

The Prince of the Geats, whose name was Beowulf, came to help the King of the Danes. Beowulf set a trap for the monster in the palace. A tremendous fight took place. During the battle, Beowulf was able to tear off one of the monster's arms. The defeated monster vanished into the lake.

Beowulf returned home and was praised as a hero. But then, news reached him that Grendel's mother had arrived at the palace to take her revenge. So Beowulf chased Grendel's mother into the lake, where he cut off her head with a magic sword!

Tired but victorious, Beowulf returned to the kingdom of the Geats. There he became king.

Fifty years went by. A monster also lived in Beowulf's kingdom, a dragon that guarded a treasure. One day, the monster began to terrorize the land.

By this time, Beowulf was an old man. But he wanted to save his kingdom. So, accompanied by his loyal friend, Wiglaf, he courageously faced the dragon. A tremendous battle took place. Wiglaf remained close to Beowulf, but the king was mortally wounded by the dragon's poison. Still he gathered all his courage and fought with all his might and . . .

Halfway through my tale, Scribblehopper stopped me. "Does this story end well?" he whispered. "I mean, it would be **good** if the dragon wins."

Oops. Maybe "Beowulf" wasn't the best story to tell a dragon. I mean, the dragon doesn't exactly **win** the fight.

I cleared my throat. "Um, Your Fiery Majesty, I think you might like another story better," I stammered.

Quickly I racked my brain, thinking of all of the dragon stories I knew.

Just then, I remembered something. In the East, dragons are symbols of *good luck*. I would tell him a Chinese legend. Then everyone would be happy.

I began to tell the tale.

Chinese character meaning "dragon"

The Princess of the Dragons
A Chinese Legend

A long time ago, in a faraway land, a poor young man went every day to the banks of the river to collect wood. One day, the waters parted and a beautiful maiden riding a red dragon appeared. She combed her hair for a long time and then disappeared back into the lake.

Hopelessly in love with her, the young man dove in and courageously swam to the bottom of the lake. To his surprise, he found the Palace of the Dragons of Fortune, which was surrounded by dry land where one could breathe. At its door, there were two dragons, a white one and a black one.

The white dragon asked, "What is the oldest thing?"

The young man answered, "Time!"

The black dragon asked, "What is the most precious thing?"

The young man answered, "Happiness!"

The two dragons smiled. "You are young, but wise!" They took him to the maiden. "I am the Princess of the Dragons," she said. "I have been waiting for you for a long time. Now you will become my husband!"

The young man returned home to his old mother and took her back with him to the bottom of the lake.

"Dress my husband and his honorable mother in silk," the young woman ordered the dragons. "Place a golden ring on each of their ten fingers. Prepare a one-hundred-course banquet for their happiness. Have a thousand musicians play to soothe their spirit."

The festivities began immediately and are still going on to this day, in the prosperous, happy, and eternal Palace of the Dragons of Fortune.

PRINCESS SCATTERBRAIN

When I was done with my story, King Firebreath clapped his claws. "**Bravo!**" he cried. Then he called for his royal niece, Princess Scatterbrain.

A mischievous-looking little dragon came **BOUNCING** up.

"My dear niece, accompany these royal guests to the border of the kingdom," he proclaimed.

Princess Scatterbrain was so excited. "Wow, Royal Uncle! That means I'll have to skip school! *What fiery good fortune!*" she chirped.

Princess Scatterbrain

"Yes, yes," King Firebreath agreed. "Speaking of school,

have you finished your geography homework?"

Princess Scatterbrain nodded. "Oh, yes!"

"Go on, then," said King Firebreath. "But remember—as soon as you reach the border, you must come back."

We took off with Princess Scatterbrain as our guide. Scribblehopper began chatting away happily. "With a guide, we'll get there *faster than a tadpole on his way to a fly bake*," he grinned.

But when I asked Princess Scatterbrain which way we were headed, she didn't sound too sure. "Oh, `this way, that way`," she muttered.

After several hours, we still weren't there and it felt as if we had been *walking in circles*!

I turned to our guide. "Tell the truth, Princess," I said sternly. "Do you know where we are?"

She hung her head. "Oh, flame fizzlers!" she sobbed. "I didn't study my geography, so I

Little Dipper

North Star

Big Dipper

It's easy to find your way using the stars. On nights without a moon, look at the sky. To find the North Star, first look for the Big Dipper. At its right you will find the Little Dipper. The brightest star below it is the North Star!

don't know. But please don't tell King Firebreath! He'll be steaming!"

Scribblehopper wrung his flippers. "We're doomed!"

Before the frog could go on, I clapped my paw over his mouth. "Don't worry," I reassured him. "We can find our way using the **STARS**. The Emerald Door is due north. All we need to do is follow the North Star. And there it is!"

What luck! I was glad I had taken that course on stargazing at New Mouse University. Before long, a glimmering green gem rose before us.

It was the Emerald Door.

THE VOICE OF THE SEA OF GRASS

As we walked through the door, once again the music box began to chime. This time, I heard the musical note *F*.

The emerald slid open. Inside was a **thin golden cord**. It was so thin it almost looked like a piece of hair or thread, or maybe some dental floss.

A sea of grass stretched out in front of us. The air was scented with flowers.

"Now, where's the map of the Kingdom of the

Pixies?" Scribblehopper huffed. "This place is so disorganized."

Just then, a beetle with a SHINY body and long pincers raced by. The map was on his belly.

Flying stag beetle

"Hey, you! Come back here!" the frog croaked. He chased the bug down. Then he stood very still. "Listen, Fair Knight," he whispered. "Can you hear it? That's the voice of the Sea of Grass."

At first, all I heard was the gentle whoosh of the breeze blowing through the grass. But then I heard something else. It sounded like "Beeeewaaare of the pixieeeees! Beeeeeware of their tricksssss!"

I scratched my head. Was the grass really talking? Or had the cheese finally slipped off my cracker?

THE MYSTERIOUS GREEN LABYRINTH

In front of us were several signposts. Each one pointed to a different path that disappeared into the tall grass.

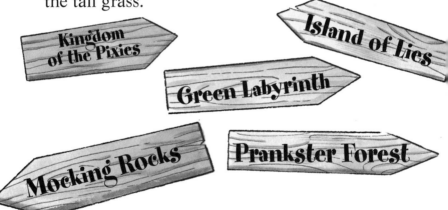

"Ooh! How exciting!" Princess Scatterbrain squealed. "I've never been in the Kingdom of the Pixies before!"

I nearly jumped out of my fur. I had forgotten the princess was still with us. "Shouldn't you

The Kingdom of the Pixies

Color: Green   **Gem:** Emerald   **Metal:** Brass

Musical Note: F

King: King Chuckles, Prince of Pranks, Lord of Tricks, King of Laughter, Emperor of Busybodies, Grandsire of Jokesters, He Who Talks in Riddles

Royal Palace: Big Bluebell

Guardian of the Kingdom: Enigma, the Green Monster of the Labyrinth. He devours anyone who does not answer his riddles correctly.

Currency of the Kingdom: Pranky franc

Spoken Language: Pixan

History of Its Inhabitants: There are many types of pixies. Most are friendly and mischievous. Every country of the world has their own pixies. For example, the Alven are Dutch pixies who travel on soap bubbles. The Bergfolk are Scandinavian pixies who mix soup with their long noses. The Brownie is an Irish pixie who helps with chores.

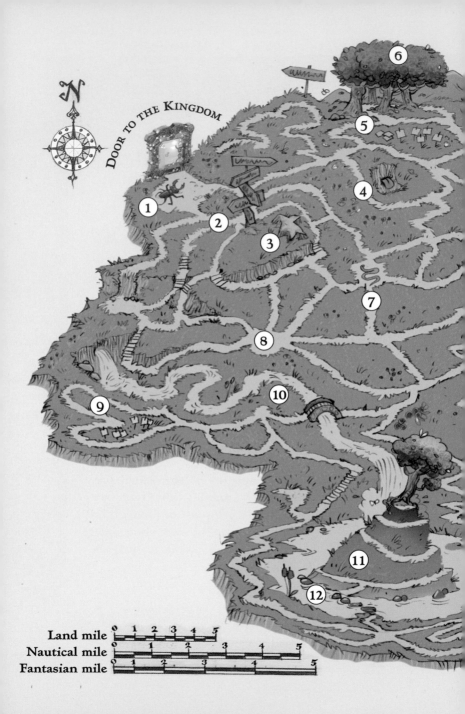

DOOR TO THE KINGDOM

Land mile

Nautical mile

Fantasian mile

The Kingdom of the Pixies

return home, like your uncle said?" I squeaked.

But Princess Scatterbrain just giggled. Then she ran off.

We chased after the little dragon until she disappeared into a green maze of hedges.

"Fire-roasted fruit flies! It's the Green Labyrinth!" Scribblehopper screeched.

I was about to ask him about the labyrinth when a cry filled the air.

"**Help!**" Princess Scatterbrain shrieked. "He's got me!"

In front of the maze was a welcome sign. It read:

WELCOME, ONE AND ALL!

COME ON IN! DON'T BE SHY! BE OUR

GUEST! MAKE YOURSELVES AT HOME!

EVERYONE CAN GO RIGHT IN . . . BUT NO ONE EVER FINDS THEIR WAY OUT!

How nice, I thought. This creature certainly seemed to like guests. Then Scribblehopper grabbed my paw. He pointed to the tiny print at the bottom of the sign.

My teeth began to chatter. I twisted my tail up in a knot. Oh, why did Princess Scatterbrain have to get lost in this creepy maze?

What could we do? We ran after the princess.

In a matter of minutes, we were hopelessly lost.

THE RIDDLE TOURNAMENT

At last, we found our way to the center of the **MAZE**. There was a well in the middle with a cage next to it. Inside sat Princess Scatterbrain. "Yoo-hoo, friends!" she called. "Watch out for the big green monster."

Scribblehopper turned pale. "She's talking about **Enigma**," he explained. "He's the ferocious green monster that guards the Labyrinth. He lives down in the well, and he'll only let us leave if we can answer his riddles."

Suddenly, a dry, scaly green arm burst out of the well and a voice hissed out the first question.

Enigma

An enigma is a question, often written in verse, that is difficult to answer. The most famous is the riddle of the Sphinx.

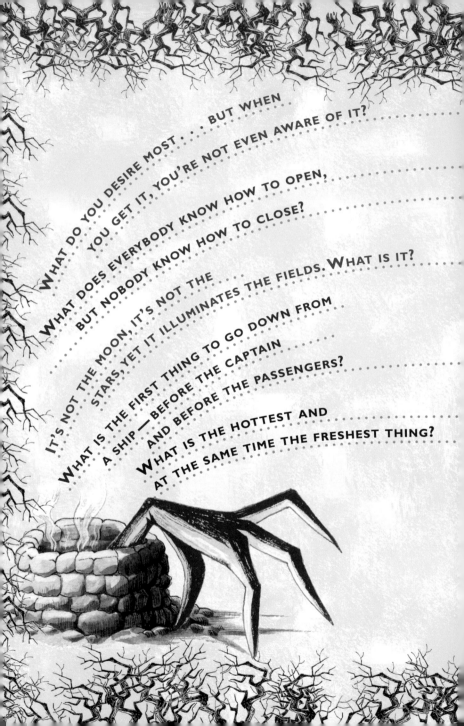

WHAT DO YOU DESIRE MOST . . . BUT WHEN YOU GET IT, YOU'RE NOT EVEN AWARE OF IT?

WHAT DOES EVERYBODY KNOW HOW TO OPEN, BUT NOBODY KNOW HOW TO CLOSE?

IT'S NOT THE MOON, IT'S NOT THE STARS, YET IT ILLUMINATES THE FIELDS. WHAT IS IT?

WHAT IS THE FIRST THING TO GO DOWN FROM A SHIP — BEFORE THE CAPTAIN AND BEFORE THE PASSENGERS?

WHAT IS THE HOTTEST AND AT THE SAME TIME THE FRESHEST THING?

Bread!

The anchor!

A lightning bug!

An egg!

Sleep!

THE CHALLENGE OF ILLUSIONS

Enigma challenged me to a tournament of optical ILLUSIONS. They were all very strange. But luckily I managed to win this challenge paws down!

Optical Illustions

An optical illusion is an image that tricks you because it appears different than what it really is!

These two arches are the same length, even if they do not seem to be!

These two lines are the same length, even though they do not appear to be!

The two horizontal lines are the same length, but they don't look it!

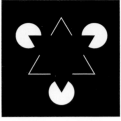

Do you see a black triangle in the middle of the box? It's only an optical illusion!

Do you see a white square in the middle of the box? It's only an optical illusion!

Do you see a white goblet or two black faces in profile? It's an optical illusion!

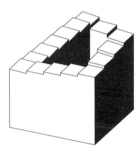

Try to follow the steps. It will seem like you are always going down!

It seems that this object has three points!

The impossible triangle: The angles look three-dimensional, but they are only two!

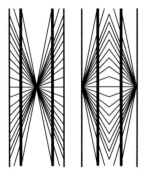

The two vertical lines are parallel, even if they don't look that way!

The diagonal white lines are parallel, even if they don't appear to be!

Help! My tongue is all twisted!

THE TOURNAMENT OF TONGUE TWISTERS

Tongue Twister
A sentence that contains words in a row that are hard to pronounce.

Finally, Enigma challenged me to a tournament of tongue twisters. Luckily for me, I won.

HOW MUCH WOOD COULD A WOODCHUCK CHUCK IF A WOODCHUCK COULD CHUCK WOOD?

SHE SELLS SEASHELLS BY THE SEASHORE.

PETER PIPER PICKED A PECK OF PICKLED PEPPERS.

BETTY BOTTER BOUGHT A BIT OF BUTTER TO PUT INTO HER BATTER.

Enigma freed Princess Scatterbrain. Then he led us out of the Labyrinth.

Princess Scatterbrain was overjoyed. "You two are **SIZZLING**!" she told us. I think that meant she liked us.

We decided to make her a member of the *Order of the Fairy Queen*. Now we had four members: Scribblehopper, myself, Princess Scatterbrain, and Shelly. Oh, I know Shelly couldn't come with us, but Scribblehopper and I agreed she would always be a **member**.

We set off toward the royal palace of the Pixies in an excellent mood. But after an hour, we found ourselves right back where we'd started. The **Mischievous Signs** had tricked us! They'd spun us around like tops!

GNIK SELKCUHC

We stood under a big blue flower, deciding what to do next.

All of a sudden, Scribblehopper leaped up.

"Jumping tadpoles!" he croaked, pointing to the flower. "It's *Big Bluebell*, the royal palace of the prankster pixies!"

I saw a little creature smirking at us. He was dressed all in green, with tiny shoes made of tree bark. It was Chuckles, the King of the Pixies.

"Uoy era os hsiloof!" he said.

"I wonder if he speaks English," Scribblehopper whispered.

Chuckles chuckled. Then he spoke again. "Ho, tahw a hcnub fo spoopmocnin!" he snickered. Then he scribbled a few words on a sheet of paper.

THE PRANKSTER PIXIES' COURT
Made up of Mischievous Advisers to the King

"I ma Gnik fo eht Seixip!" it read.

I looked at the sheet of paper. At last, I understood.

"My name is Stilton, *Geronimo Stilton*," I said. "And I've discovered your secret: You speak backward!"

"Os, Notlits si ruoy eman?" King Chuckles said. "Er'uoy a thgink, s'taht raelc. Won llet em yhw uoy era ereh."

I was going to tell King Chuckles that I wasn't a knight, but then I thought, why bother? So

instead I pulled out the GOLDEN string from in the music box.

King Chuckles's eyes gleamed. He grabbed the string and attached it to a tiny violin. Then he began to play. *ZIN...ZIN...ZINNNN!*

Suddenly, I felt the irresistible urge to dance. How strange! It was as if some strange power had taken over my paws.

The King of the Pixies forced us to dance for two hours. Finally, King Chuckles put down his violin.

I FLOPPED to the floor. "Please, Your Majesty," I gasped. "Blossom, the Queen of the Fairies, is in danger. We need to leave your kingdom as soon as possible!"

King Chuckles roared with laughter. "Reven!" he cried.

Never? I gulped.

I was at least hoping for a "**maybe**."

Right then, Scribblehopper told me the King of the Pixies always did the opposite of what was asked. "Actually, we want to stay **forever**," I said. "We want to eat here. We want to sleep here. We want to watch the grass grow here until we're old and gray."

King Chuckles knit his brow. Then he screeched, "Od uoy yllaer tnaw ot yats? Neht ll'I evird uoy yawa! A ediug lliw ekat uoy morf ym dnal! Kciuq! Hctef eno rof siht yllis dnab!"

Cheesecake! We were on our way!

TODAY, MY NAME'S TRICK!

The pixie who was to be our guide skipped over to us. "Welcome to the Order of the Fairy Queen," I said. "With you, that makes five of us. What's your name?"

The pixie winked. "We pixies have a special tradition: We change our names every day. Today my name is **TRICK**. Tomorrow it might be **CRICK**. Or **SKIP** or **FLIP**. Or **WICK** or **STICK**," he laughed.

Princess Scatterbrain stepped up. "Excuse me,"

she said. "But which way should we head to reach the Sapphire Door?"

Trick made a face. Then he began hopping around the little dragon. "Here or there. I don't care. Now shut your snout, you smelly trout!" he sneered.

Princess Scatterbrain snorted out a flame. "How dare you talk to me that way!" she yelled. "I am a royal dragon!"

Trick giggled and said,

"Royal, schmoil! Don't put on that pout.
You're just a little sausage snout.
If you're a princess, then I'm a king.
And rocks can laugh and dance and sing!"

THE PIXIE TREE

Trick skipped around and around. Then he **vanished** under the leaf-covered branches of an oak tree. I heard lots and lots of voices within the tree. I wondered how many pixies were hiding there. (There are **seven** of them! Can you find them all?)

Just then, Trick sprang out from behind the tree. He skipped over the grass and shrieked. But Scribblehopper caught him under his hat.

"I'm so sneaky. Hee, hee, hee. You can never ever catch me!"

Got you, you little rascal!

We are small
but mischievous.

We are pesky.
Who are we?

"Now, tell us where the Sapphire Door is!" he demanded.

Trick did a somersault. Then he stuck out his tongue. At last, he giggled,

"You really, really want to know? The Sapphire Door is right here, by your toe!"

He pointed to a large mushroom by our feet.

Scribblehopper was fuming. "What? The Sapphire Door was right here the whole time, and you didn't tell us?" he screeched.

As I was trying to calm everyone down, we passed through the Sapphire Door!

The Door to the Kingdom of the Gnomes

Look at all the beautiful trees and colors!

BLACKBERRIES, RASPBERRIES, AND HUCKLEBERRIES

As we crossed through the door, the music box chimed. This time, it was the musical note *G*.

The sapphire opened up. Inside, I saw two tiny gold wedding rings.

The sunlight GLINTED off the rings. I looked up. We were standing in the middle of a patch of freshly plowed land. I lay down on the warm earth. Don't you just love the smell of rich soil? I do. It reminds me of my great-great-great-grandmother Hearty Paws's farm. She grows all her own vegetables. Then she uses them to make

some _whisker-_
licking good
meals. Yum!

We discovered
the map of the
Kingdom of
the Gnomes
hanging from a tree.

Scribblehopper grabbed it, and we continued on
our way. We hiked through a beautiful forest.
Squirrels and rabbits scampered along the path in
front of us. The LEAVES crackled crisply
beneath our feet. I closed my eyes and breathed
in the fresh, clean air. I felt so refreshed. I felt so
alive. I felt so . . . hungry.

CRACKLE CRACKLE CRACKLE CRACKLE CRACKLE CRACKLE CRACKLE CRACKLE

Rats! I should have tried the pixie plum pie back at Big Bluebell. I sighed. Just then Trick tumbled right into a huge berry patch. Cheesecake! We munched away happily on delicious blackberries, raspberries, and huckleberries. Princess Scatterbrain pointed out a **GIANT** strawberry beneath a chestnut tree. Its scent was so strong and sweet. We felt drawn to it. But the moment we touched it, an enormous net captured us! We were lifted into the air and WHISKED AWAY through the woods!

What was going on? I felt sick. Maybe I shouldn't have eaten that last huckleberry.

"Don't worry, Geronimo of Stilton," Scribblehopper said reassuringly. "This is just the gnomes' NO HASSLE CREATURE CARRIER. It's taking us to their royal palace. You'll see that the gnomes are very wise, and they *love* everyone."

The Kingdom of the Gnomes

Color: Light Blue   **Gem:** Sapphire   **Metal:** Tin

Musical Note: G

King: King Factual, nature lover, protector of all animals great and small, wise and gentle bookworm

Queen: Queen Cozy, the cheerful cook and mother hen

Royal Palace: Big Bark Lodge

Guardian of the Kingdom: No Hassle Creature Carrier, a contraption that carries visitors to Big Bark Lodge

Currency of the Kingdom: Gnomic rubles

Spoken Language: Gnomeeze

History of Its Inhabitants: The name *gnome* comes from *gnomizio*, which is an ancient Greek word meaning, "I know." Gnomes know the mysteries of nature. Defenders of the rights of plants and animals, gnomes live underground among the roots of centuries-old trees. They always have an excellent disposition and they love funny stories. They adore reading. No more than three inches tall, they become adults at three years of age and live to be more than three hundred years old.

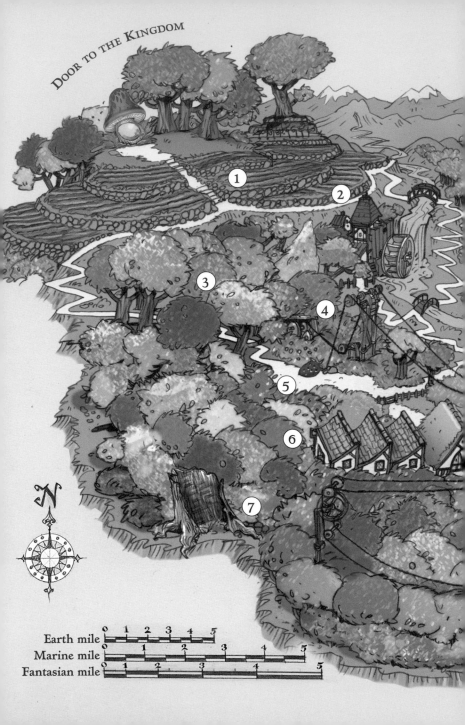

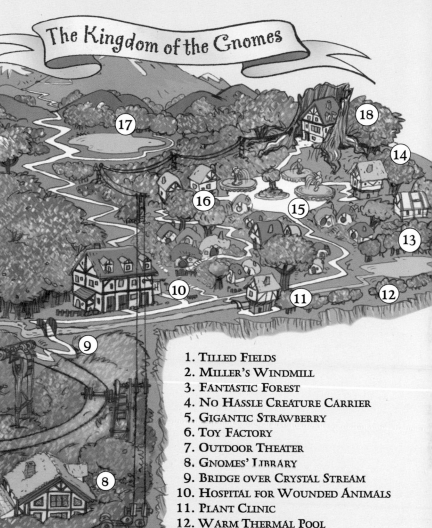

The Kingdom of the Gnomes

1. TILLED FIELDS
2. MILLER'S WINDMILL
3. FANTASTIC FOREST
4. NO HASSLE CREATURE CARRIER
5. GIGANTIC STRAWBERRY
6. TOY FACTORY
7. OUTDOOR THEATER
8. GNOMES' LIBRARY
9. BRIDGE OVER CRYSTAL STREAM
10. HOSPITAL FOR WOUNDED ANIMALS
11. PLANT CLINIC
12. WARM THERMAL POOL
13. GNOMIC MUSEUM
14. POST OFFICE
15. THREE GNOME SQUARE
16. BAKERY AND TAILOR SHOP
17. FAWN LAKE
18. BIG BARK LODGE

THE NO HASSLE CREATURE CARRIER

The net zipped us all the way to the tiny village of the gnomes. We flew over a teeny-tiny toy factory, a clean, bright animal hospital, and a greenhouse bursting with colorful plants and flowering trees. A large waterwheel churned slowly in the river. We passed a yummy-smelling bakery and a neat little library. I wondered how many teeny-tiny books were inside.

At the center of the village stood Three Gnome Square.

For a moment, I felt a little homesick. I couldn't help thinking of Three Rat Square back in **New Mouse City**.

But before I could get too weepy, we reached a large, hollow tree. This was it — the royal palace of the gnomes, also known as **Big Bark Lodge**.

THE GNOME COURT

The net dropped us off in a big hall. The gnomes were in the middle of some type of celebration. The King of the Gnomes sat in a **LARGE** wooden chair. He was dressed in Mint green pants and an **olive green** vest. On his feet, he wore a pair of sturdy wooden clogs. A bright ORANGE cap adorned his head. He had cheerful blue eyes and *big, bushy eyebrows*.

"Interesting," the King of the Gnomes murmured. He was reading from a large book entitled *Gnome Sweet Gnome: First-aid Tips for Ailing Gnomes.*

The Queen of the Gnomes wore a dress of ORANGE wool. She had on the same clogs as her husband and the same kind of cap. She was busily knitting away.

I pulled out the two gold rings that I'd found in the music box. I was about to offer them to the couple when I slipped on the polished floor. "**Ouch!**" I squeaked, crushing my whiskers.

The Queen of the Gnomes dropped her knitting needles. "Are you hurt?" she asked with alarm.

I staggered to my feet. "Um, no, Your Majesty," I mumbled. How embarrassing!

But the Queen of the Gnomes just *giggled*. "Call me Cozy, dear," she said with a smile.

Meanwhile, the grinning King of the Gnomes hopped out of his chair.

"At last!" he cried. "I can try out my book on gnomish FIRST AID!"

He shook my paw. "King Factual's the name," he announced. "Now, do you have any bruises?"

I shook my head.

"Do you need a bandage?" he continued.

I shook my head.

"How about some nice antibiotic ointment?" he went on. "Or a HOT pack, a cold pack, or a honey throat lozenge?"

"Oh, leave the poor rodent alone, Factual," Queen Cozy piped up. "All this knight needs is some *delicious* cheese lasagna."

Before the King of the Gnomes could protest, I gave him the two gold rings.

"Well, imagine that! Today we're celebrating our **fiftieth** wedding anniversary!" King Factual chuckled. The couple thanked me from the bottom of their hearts.

THERE'S NO PLACE LIKE GNOME!

King Factual and Queen Cozy gave us a tour of the palace. Queen Cozy glowed when we reached the kitchen. I could tell it was her favorite place to be. Hanging on the walls were **SPARKLING** copper pots. Yummy-looking dishes sizzled on the stove.

The **library** was King Factual's pride and joy. "Ah, how I love my books!" He grinned. I grinned, too. How could I not love a gnome who loves his books!

QUEEN Cozy

The couple showed us the assembly hall, where the gnomes went to vote. Then we passed through

Full-belly Hall, where banquets were held, and Don't Step on My Toes, the ballroom.

The gnomes were expert mechanics. They were also friends of nature. "We use only **SOLAR** power," King Factual explained. He pointed to all of the solar panels on the roofs of the houses. They even had some solar-powered cars and airplanes.

The gnomes grew all kinds of vegetables and fruits using only **NATURAL FERTILIZER**! They were very kind to their farm animals.

They fed the cows the sweetest grass, and they

Solar panel atop a gnomic house

KING FACTUAL

Natural fertilizer!

made comfy beds of hay for the chickens.

As we walked around the village, gnomes ran up to greet us. I felt so *welcome*.

At one house, a pretty gnome invited us inside. She showed us around her house, then fed us steaming bowls of tasty gnome noodle soup. It was *whisker-licking* good!

As we waved good-bye, I noticed a plaque hanging over her door. It read: THERE'S NO PLACE LIKE GNOME.

Happy chickens lay beautiful fresh eggs!

THE SILVER SLED

After our tour, I
turned to King Factual.
"Sir, I was wondering if you
could give us a *guide* so we can
reach the Kingdom of the Giants," I asked.

"Of course!" King Factual said. "In fact, Queen
Cozy and I will be your guides."

We began walking along the **snowy** path that led to the Kingdom of the Giants. King Factual and Queen Cozy traveled on a **SILVER SLED** that was pulled by twelve white bunny rabbits.

At lunchtime, we took a break. We sat down near a crystal-clear stream. Queen Cozy handed out homemade **carrot** cake to everyone — even the rabbits.

It was delicious.

"Hope you don't think I'm being nosy, Good

Knight, but where is your armor?" Queen Cozy asked.

I told her that I didn't have any armor.

"But all knights have armor!" she cried.

I told her that I didn't have any armor because I wasn't a knight.

She shook with *laughter*.

"Oh, don't be silly. Of course you're a knight," she insisted. "It's as plain as the nose on your snout."

I stared at my reflection in the stream. What was so special about my snout?

"Oh, I get it, Knight," Queen Cozy whispered. "You have INVISIBLE armor, right? Don't worry. Your secret is safe with me."

Oh, **why** didn't anyone ever believe me?

A FEAST FIT FOR EVERYONE

We traveled through the snow for the rest of the day. Finally, King Factual brought the sled to a halt near a Waterfall.

"Hmm. Based on the distance we have traveled, my compass, and the direction of the sun, it looks like we're here," he announced. "Yes, there's the Amethyst Door! Am I good or what?"

Queen Cozy rolled her eyes. "Now let's get down to the really important stuff — food," she said.

She began rummaging through the bottom of the sled. Then she pulled out a **FEAST** fit for a king, a queen, a mouse, a frog, a pixie, and a dragon. It was incredible!

There were **fresh bread**, potato dumplings, stuffed **zucchini**, hot cheese buns, onion soup, apple **pie**, and more.

With a puff, Princess Scatterbrain lit the fire. Trick and I set the table. The plates and glasses were so perfect and tiny. And the food was so tasty.

We made a toast with huckleberry juice.

"To good friends, big and small!" we cheered.

Then I asked if anyone wanted to hear a story about gnomes.

Everyone did. So I began to tell the story.

THE GNOMES' THREE SMALL MAGIC STONES
A Norwegian legend

One day, Thorstein, a very strong warrior, sailed off in search of adventure. On top of a cliff, he saw a gnome crying. "A bird of prey has snatched my wife!"

Thorstein looked up and saw a tiny dot in the clouds. He pointed his arrow and hit the bird, which plunged to the ground.

The little lady gnome fell from the bird's claws. The warrior caught her and brought her to her husband. The husband was overjoyed.

"You are a great warrior, and I am only a small gnome. But I want to offer you a gift to show my appreciation," he said.

He gave the warrior three small stones: a white one, a yellow one, and a red one.

"The white one is to make snow. The yellow one is to make the sun shine. The red one is to make a lightning bolt."

The warrior traveled on until he ran into a gigantic ogre. "I will eat you up with one gulp!" the ogre said. Thorstein took out the little white stone, and it began to snow very heavily. The ogre shivered.

Then the warrior took out the little yellow stone, and the burning sun melted all the snow, which turned into a river. The ogre was engulfed by the raging water. Finally, the warrior took out the little red stone. The ogre was struck by the lightning bolt. He crumbled to ashes.

The warrior placed the little stones in his pocket and smiled. The gnome's little gift had saved his life.

King Factual and Queen Cozy loved the story. "Maybe we can help you. May we join the *Order of the Fairy Queen*?" they asked.

Scribblehopper hopped up and down. "Surfing salamanders! With you, that makes **seven** of us!" he croaked happily.

And so, together, *we walked through the Amethyst Door.*

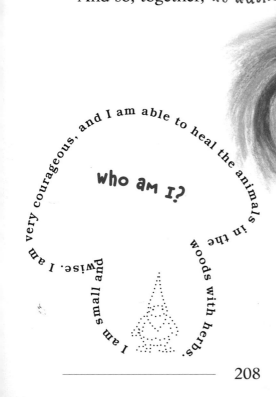

who am I?

and I am able to heal the animals in the woods with herbs. I am small and pwise. I am very courageous,

The Door to the Kingdom of the Giants

Brrrr! What a cold climate!

THE LAND OF THE NEVER-ENDING SNOWFLAKES

Once again, a musical note tinkled. It was an
a. The amethyst in the music box lifted up.

Beneath it, I saw a word engraved in the Fantasian alphabet. I wondered what it said. But I was too cold to worry about it. That's because we were standing in the middle of snow-covered mountains. The **icy** air stung our lungs. Cheese niblets! I was freezing my tail off!

"It's always **WINTER** in the icy Kingdom of the Giants," King Factual explained. "Some call it the Land of the Never-ending Snowflakes."

I shivered. Don't get me wrong, I like snowflakes as much as the next rodent. I just like them when I'm inside my mouse hole drinking a nice cup of hot cheddar.

Before long, we discovered the map of the Kingdom of the Giants. It was sculpted on a piece of granite. The gnomes, the toad, and I studied the map. Princess Scatterbrain and Trick were busy playing with a large pinecone. The pinecone **rolled** down a hill, and they ran after it. That's when disaster struck.

The pinecone settled in the middle of a frozen lake. When Princess Scatterbrain tried to reach it, she crashed right through the ice! Talk about an ice breaker!

Luckily, we formed a chain and were able to pull out our friend.

Heeeeeeeeelp!

The Kingdom of the Giants

Color: Indigo   **Gem:** Amethyst   **Metal:** Titanium

Musical Note: A

King: Unfortunately, there is no longer a king in the Kingdom of the Giants. But when there was, he was called King of the Knights, Protector of the Truth, Defender of the Damsels in Distress, Governor of Generosity.

Royal Palace: Falcon's Beak

Guardian of the Kingdom: The year-round glaciers covering the mountains in this kingdom

Currency of the Kingdom: Gigantic ruble

Spoken Language: Gigantesque

History of Its Inhabitants: According to Greek legends, the giants were brought to life to avenge the Titans, who had been imprisoned by Zeus. Famous giants include Goliath, whose name means "all the enemies of the Earth;" Polyphemus, a one-eyed Cyclops; Yspaddaden, whose look could paralyze an entire army; and Vipunen, also known as "Guardian of Enchantments."

DOOR TO THE KINGDOM

The Kingdom of the Giants

1. PEAK OF PURITY
2. LAKE OF WILLINGNESS
3. MOUNTAIN OF COURAGE
4. PEAK OF STRENGTH
5. ROAD OF THE ANCIENT KINGS
6. MOUNTAIN OF PRIDE
7. MOUNTAIN OF HONOR
8. EXCALIBUR
9. GENEROSITY RIVER
10. DEN OF THE BEAR WHO SAVED THE GIANT
11. HOT THERMAL SPRINGS
12. FALCON'S BEAK, THE ROYAL PALACE OF THE GIANTS
13. PEAK OF HOPE
14. MOUNTAIN OF WHITE FURY
15. MOUNTAIN OF COMPASSION
16. PEAK OF FORGIVENESS

ON THE ROAD OF THE ANCIENT KINGS

Princess Scatterbrain was so cold, she couldn't breathe *FIRE* for ten whole minutes.

Finally, we started off again along a white gravel road. Massive statues of proud warriors stared down at us as we passed by.

"This is the Road of the Ancient Kings. Once there were many members of the royal family, but now they're all gone. There is no one to wear the crown of the King of the Giants," Scribblehopper told us.

Suddenly, I noticed a **GIANT** shadow among the statues.

"Who is it?" I shouted, trembling.

But no one answered. My whiskers quivered with fear.

"W-who is it? W-w-who's there?" I stammered.

Just then, someone pinched my tail. Was it a monster? Was it a giant? Was it a giant monster?

Suddenly, I heard a *teeny-tiny* laugh. I whipped around. It was that pesky pixie, Trick, again! He'd been playing tricks on me ever since I'd met him. Now he tied my tail up in a knot. Then he stuck his tongue out at me.

"Look at the knight. Oh, what a sight! He's shaking with fear. It's perfectly clear!" he teased, running off.

I was steaming. That was it. It was time to put my paw down. I was sick and tired of Trick's annoying pranks. I took off after him.

My friends cheered me on. "Go get him, Knight!" they called.

"TEACH HIM A LESSON!" they shouted.

The pixie thumbed his nose at us. He hopped up onto one of the statues. He climbed up the warrior's horse and tiptoed out to the tip of his sword.

"You can't catch me, Furry Snout! All you can do is cry and pout!" Trick sneered.

I gnashed my teeth together. I was ready to shake him. I was ready to squeeze him. But was I ready to risk my neck to save him?

The pixie had slipped! He was dangling off the statue from his hat!

"Help!" he squealed. "I'm going to fall!"

I started to climb up the statue. But at the top, I remembered something: I'm afraid of heights!

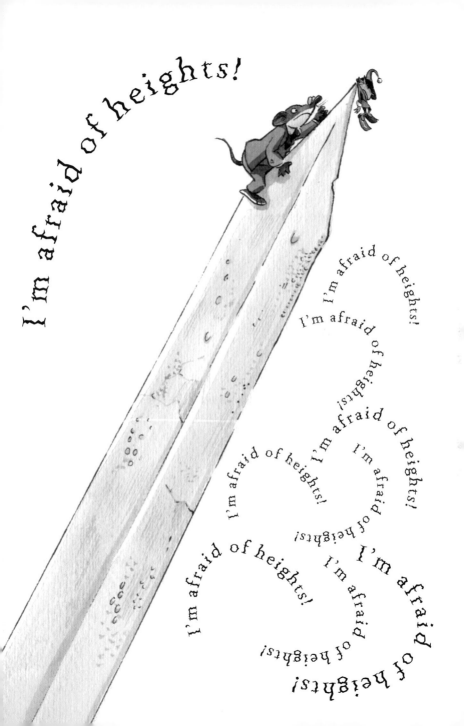

Pixie Jam

"**BE CAREFUL**, Sir Geronimo!" Scribblehopper cried.

I looked down. My friends looked so tiny. Holey cheese! I was practically touching the CLOUDS! My paws began to shake. Sweat poured from my fur. Oh, why did I climb up so high? I wasn't a monkey. I was a mouse. Correction: I was a scaredy mouse!

"Please save me!" Trick begged. "If I fall, I'll be nothing but pixie jam!"

What could I do? Even though the pixie was a pest, he didn't deserve to be turned into preserves.

At last, I reached the very top of the statue. "Give me your hand, **QUICK**!" I told the pixie. I grabbed him just before his cap ripped in two.

We carefully climbed back down. As soon as we reached the ground, Trick threw his tiny arms around me. Then he sang a song to me.

"You are so gentle
and kind and brave.
I'll never forget
that my life
you did save!"

ANYONE CAN SAY THEY'RE A KNIGHT

We left the statues behind us and continued traveling. At last, we reached the top of the Mountain of White Fury. We searched for the Diamond Door that would lead us to the Kingdom of the Fairies. But there was so much **SNOW** it was hard to see. Plus, with every pawstep, I sank further d o w n into the powdery drifts.

It was then that I noticed another set of **pawprints**. Well, they weren't exactly pawprints. They were more like a giant set of footprints.

"Are you **sure** that no one lives in this kingdom?" I asked the frog.

Before he could answer me, everything went fuzzy. A strong gust of wind sent my glasses flying. I was as blind as my grouchy grandma Onewhisker before her cataract surgery.

I began to feel around in the snow for my glasses. All of a sudden, I touched something Soft and hairy. I gulped. Something told me it wasn't a cute snow bunny. Just then, I found my glasses. I put them on and nearly fainted. I was holding on to the **red** beard of a giant!

I let go and tumbled back into a snowdrift. *Maybe if I play dead,*

THE GIANT'S BEARD

THE GIANT'S SHOE

the giant will go away, I thought. At that moment, a giant shoe stepped on me.

"**Help!**" I squeaked. "I'm not dead. It was just an act!"

The shoe moved. "Sorry," a loud but kind voice said. "I didn't see you."

THE GIANT'S HAND

Put me down!

The giant picked me up by my tail and dangled me in the air! Two **blue** eyes stared at me curiously.

"Who are you?" the giant asked.

Scribblehopper spoke up. "Can't you see? *He's* a knight in shining armor, of course. He's come to save the Queen of the Fairies," he croaked.

My whiskers curled up in frustration. "For the last time, Scibblehopper, I am **NOT** a knight!" I cried. "My name is Stilton, *Geronimo Stilton*!"

The giant thought this over. "Hmmm . . . Anyone can say they're a knight," he said. "How many tournaments have you won? How many damsels in distress have you **SAVED**? And where's your suit of shining armor?"

I tried to explain that I wasn't a **KNIGHT**. I just wanted to help the Queen of the Fairies.

"Save a *queen*. Yes, that's something a knight would do," he muttered.

Meanwhile King Factual and Queen Cozy introduced themselves and asked the giant to join us on our journey.

The giant **SCRATCHED** his head. "Hmmm . . . Anyone can say they're going on a journey. Where are you going? How long will it take? Are you bringing a **bathrobe** and a pair of *slippers*?" he asked.

As they were talking, Trick discovered a hot thermal spring.

"I'm going for a swim!" the pixie announced.

The giant chewed his lip. "Hmm . . . Anyone can say they're going for a swim. Do you have a **BATHING SUIT**? Are you going to dive in or jump in? Will you do the backstroke or tread water?" he asked.

Princess Scatterbrain rolled her eyes. "Okay, this is, like, sizzling my brain cells. I'm going to take a snooze," she grumbled.

The giant knit his eyebrows. "Hmm . . . Anyone can say they're taking a snooze. Did you bring a **pillow**? Do you need a blanket? How about an ALARM CLOCK?" he asked.

I closed my eyes. I couldn't take it anymore. I felt like we all were caught in a never-ending game of Giant Jeopardy.

Fortunately, at that very moment, Queen Cozy decided to make lunch.

THE LAST
OF THE GIANTS

The air filled with the delicious smell of toasted cheese. I sighed. There's nothing like a yummy toasted **cheese** sandwich after you've been stepped on by a giant.

Queen Cozy laid the sandwiches on plates. Then she offered each of us a glass of *lemonade*.

"Fresh squeezed," she declared.

The giant sniffed his drink. "Hmm . . . Anyone can say their lemonade is fresh-squeezed. When did you squeeze it? How long did it take? Did you use a juicer?" he asked.

The Queen of the Gnomes turned **purple**. She looked like she wanted to stick the giant in her juicer.

While King Factual calmed down Queen Cozy,

I turned to the giant. "You still haven't told us your name," I said.

The giant showed us a ring with a falcon on it.

THE GIANT'S RING

"I belong to the royal house of Falcon's Beak. But I don't have a first name anymore. I forgot it when I lost everyone I loved," he said, wiping away a giant tear.

I pulled an **UMBRELLA** out of my backpack. After all, who wants to drown in someone else's tear?

Luckily, the giant wasn't offended. He went on with his story. It seemed the giant was the youngest of twelve brothers. For years, they lived happily at Falcon's Beak. Then one day, there was a terrible AVALANCHE.

The family was buried alive in their castle.

ONLY THE GIANT SURVIVED. A mother bear dug him out of the ice and raised him with her cubs. Well, that explained the I LOVE HONEY T-shirt he was wearing.

"Then one day I met him," the giant continued, pointing behind me. I looked around, nervously. I didn't want another giant foot stepping on me by accident. But no giant showed up. Instead, a magnificent **falcon** appeared. It landed on the giant's arm.

"I found it with a broken wing," said the giant. "When it got better, I set it free. But it wouldn't

THE BEAR WHO SAVED THE GIANT

leave me. We've been friends ever since."

Have you ever seen a falcon? They are amazing birds. And this one was smiling!

THE GIANT'S FALCON

BATHROOMS ALL OVER THE PLACE

The giant patted the falcon's wing. Then he went on with his story. "I live in an immense mansion," he said. "It's so **BIG** it would take me a whole month to sleep in every bedroom. And forget about the bathrooms. They're all over the place."

Wow! The giant's place sounded fabumouse. I was dying to take a nice hot bath. The word *bathroom* made me daydream about cheesy-scented bath bubbles. Suddenly the giant burst into tears. Nothing like a few tears to burst my **bubbles**!

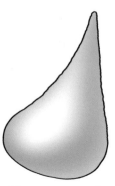

THE GIANT'S TEAR

"Oh, it is so sad, living alone in such a huge house," the giant sobbed. "I have lost everything. My family, my friends, even my name."

Try to decipher the giant's name!

Just then, I remembered something. A word was engraved beneath the amethyst. I told the giant what it was.

The giant liked the name very much.

"Now you aren't alone anymore, friend," I said. "You can join us. You can be part of the *Order of the Fairy Queen*."

Everyone cheered. The giant was so thrilled he gave me a hug. I tried not to pay attention to the bones crunching under my fur.

To celebrate our newest member, I decided to tell a **story**. It was a nice story about giants.

And this is how it went.

BRAINS OVER BRAWN
An Irish legend

In Ireland, there lived a giant who was known for his great strength. His name was Finn McCool.

One day, another giant named Cuchulain, who thought he was the strongest giant in the world, came to Finn's village. Cuchulain had a secret: His strength was concentrated in the index finger of his right hand.

The giant yelled out, "Finn McCool, where are you? I am here to challenge you!"

Finn was worried, but his wife, Oonagh, said, "Don't worry about it, I'll think of a way to take care of Cuchulain!"

Finn shook his head, "What can you do to help me? You are just a weak woman!"

Oonagh reassured him, "Brains over brawn!"

The giantess had her husband lie in a baby's crib. She told him to be still and quiet. Then she baked two loaves of bread. In one of them, she hid a rock.

When Cuchulain arrived, the sly Oonagh came out to greet him. "Are you looking for my husband, Finn McCool?" she asked. "Don't you worry, he'll be back soon. But while you're here, would you do me a favor? The sun is about to rise. Would you please turn my house in that direction? My husband does this every morning."

With a tremendous strain, Cuchulain turned the house. In the meantime, he thought, *Hmmm, this Finn McCool must be very strong!*

Then the giantess offered Cuchulain the loaf with the hidden rock. "Taste it, it's my specialty!"

As soon as the giant bit into it, he broke a tooth. "Aaaaaaaaaaaaaaaaahhhhhhhhhhh!"

The giantess feigned surprise. "Don't you like it? I always give this bread to my baby!"

In the meantime, she gave Finn McCool, who was in the crib, the bread without the rock. And Finn McCool ate it without a problem.

Meanwhile, Cuchulain was thinking, *Wow, that baby is huge! I wonder how big his father must be! He must have some phenomenal teeth!* Then he stretched his right index finger toward Finn's lips. With one chomp, Finn cleanly bit off the giant's finger.

Cuchulain screamed, "Ooooooooouuuuhhhhhhhhhh! My index finger! That was my favorite finger!"

He ran and ran and ran and never, ever, ever came back.

Finn McCool climbed out of the crib. "So what is worth more, brains or brawn?" Oonagh asked him.

Finn embraced his wife with admiration. "Woman, you should be proud of yourself. You just defeated the strongest giant in Ireland!"

AVALANCHE!

Just as I finished my story, the mountain began to tremble. I heard the distant sound of thunder. "**Avalanche!**" shouted the giant.

Holey cheese! A raging ball of snow was headed right for us!

The giant scooped us up. Seconds later,

he carried us through the Diamond Door.

THE ROSE OF A THOUSAND PETALS

At last, we had reached the Kingdom of the Fairies! I was so excited I felt like squeaking. Instead, I listened to the music box chiming. It trilled out the musical note *B*. The diamond on the music box lit up with a PURE WHITE LIGHT. A plant magically appeared. It blossomed into a *beautiful white rose* with a thousand petals. In the center of the rose appeared the map of the Kingdom of the Fairies.

The Kingdom of the Fairies

Color: Violet **Gem:** Diamond **Metal:** Silver

Musical Note: B

Queen: Blossom of the Flower, the White Queen, the Lady of Happiness, She Who Brings Harmony and Peace

Royal Palace: Crystal Castle

Guardian of the Kingdom: No one. In the Kingdom of the Fairies, there is no need to defend oneself, because no one ever offends anyone.

Currency of the Kingdom: Magical florien

Spoken Language: Fairese

History of Its Inhabitants: The word *fairy* comes from the Latin *fatum*, which means "destiny." In Gaelic, fairies are called *Daoine Sidhe*, which means "people of the hills." They sail on white boats in the shape of swans. They are talented dancers, and their song fills hearts with joy. They weave the rays of the sun and the moon on precious looms made of gold. They nourish themselves with the perfume of the flowers. They can read thoughts and communicate without words.

1. ROSE OF A THOUSAND PETALS
2. GLITTERING LAKE
3. WOODS OF GOODNESS
4. PRETTY-SHADE PLAIN
5. PINK FOREST
6. TOOTH FAIRY'S MANOR
7. TURQUOISE HOUSE
8. FLOWERY MOUNTAIN
9. SWEET-SMELLING WOODS
10. FOUNTAIN OF YOUTH
11. RARE GLADE
12. HOUSE OF THE SUN AND THE MOON
13. HOUSE THAT SINGS
14. WHISTLING WOODS
15. SILVER ABYSS
16. FAIRY GODMOTHER'S TOWER
17. SILVER-VOICED NIGHTINGALES
18. MOUNTAIN OF SWEET DREAMS
19. VALLEY OF THE BLUE UNICORNS
20. MOUNTAIN OF SECRETS
21. GAZEBO OF LOVE
22. CRYSTAL CASTLE
23. PEGASUS'S ROCK
24. SWEETWATER LAKE
25. FOREST OF THE NYMPHS
26. PETAL WAY

The Kingdom of the Fairies

19

20

24

23

22

21

25

26

Earth mile   0 1 2 3 4 5

Marine mile   0 1 2 3 4 5

Fantasian mile   0 1 2 3 4 5

THE FOUNTAIN
OF YOUTH

We followed the map to the Fountain of Youth. It was a magical waterfall surrounded by golden rocks. According to the legend, anyone who drank its ꅐꍏꋖꑾꋪ became young again.

I thought about what it was like to be a baby mouselet. Before I took my first pawstep. Before I learned how to squeak. Before I read my first newspaper from cover to cover. I must have been

On the Fountain of Youth, there is a warning written in the Fantasian alphabet.

To decipher it, go to page 315: You will find the secret code.

bored out of my fur! Plus, as a baby I couldn't even enjoy a nice slice of my favorite yummy cheddar pizza. I was stuck drinking my cheese from a bottle!

"I don't think I'd like to be *young* again," I said, patting my fur. "I like me just the way I am, *whiskers* and all!"

King Factual nodded, stroking his white beard. "I'm with you, Knight," he laughed.

THE VALLEY OF THE BLUE UNICORNS

We began walking again. Before long, we reached the Valley of the Blue Unicorns. I saw a horse with blue fur and a silver horn on its forehead.

"It's a **UNICORN**!" I squeaked excitedly.

"Hello, my name is QUICKSILVER," he said. "Have you come to save the Queen of the Fairies? If so, you must hurry. Cackle, the Queen of the Witches, is on her way!"

Scribblehopper sighed. "Sir Geronimo, I don't think I can hop another step," he said with a yawn. The others nodded in agreement.

Quicksilver seemed to understand. With a nod of his head, he summoned the other **UNICORNS** who lived in the valley. "We'll take you there. Get on our backs," he said.

Each member of the Order of the Fairy Queen climbed up on a unicorn. The unicorns had such wonderful names. There was

BLUE ARROW, SWIFT WIND, GOLDEN HOOF, BUSHY TAIL, WINGS OF BREEZE, FINE HORN, FLUFFY CLOUD, AND MAGICAL MANE.

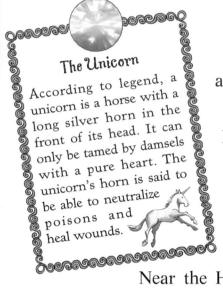

The Unicorn

According to legend, a unicorn is a horse with a long silver horn in the front of its head. It can only be tamed by damsels with a pure heart. The unicorn's horn is said to be able to neutralize poisons and heal wounds.

I climbed onto Quicksilver and we took off.

We crossed through the Pretty-shade Plain. Then we headed through Flowery Mountain. I felt like I was in the middle of the world's biggest florist shop.

Near the House of the Sun and the Moon, we spotted another beautiful sight. Flocks of nightingales soared overhead.

NIGHTINGALE WITH A SILVER VOICE

HOUSE OF THE SUN AND THE MOON

PEGASUS, THE WINGED HORSE

Just then, I saw a white horse flying in the sky. It was Pegasus. Do you know who he is? He is a horse with wings!

I was still watching the horse when I noticed something else in the sky. It was a mysterious green fog. It filled the air. I wondered what it could be. But there was no time to think about it. We had reached Sweet-smelling Woods.

I thanked Quicksilver. Then I hopped off his back.

Thank you, my friend!

THE MYSTERIOUS GREEN FOG

The sun was setting just as we reached Crystal Castle. Too bad I could barely see my own whiskers. No, I wasn't going blind.

The mysterious green fog was getting thicker and thicker!

Suddenly, I noticed a speck of blinking light fluttering in front of me.

"Psst, Knight! Oh, yoo-hoo! Your Knightliness!" a little voice called.

A firefly rested on my paw. "Hope I didn't

The firefly Blinkette

blind you with my light. Sometimes I don't know my own *wattage*," the firefly chirped. "I'm Blinkette. I just wanted to warn you about the green fog. It is a spell cast by

Cackle. It has spread throughout the Kingdom of the Fairies."

I was confused. "A spell?" I muttered. "Cackle?"

Blinkette explained that one night when the moon was full, the Queen of the Witches stirred up an evil potion in her cauldron. It was made of a thousand rare ingredients.

Holey cheese! So that's what I had seen boiling in the cauldron near Cackle's throne. It was the mysterious green fog! Blinkette listed the ingredients: *white bat wings, sand viper scales, vampire teeth, mandrake root, tarantula legs* . . . What a complicated recipe. I guess Cackle was into gourmet **POISONS**.

"The green fog has surrounded Crystal Castle," Blinkette continued. "Blossom, the Queen of the Fairies, has fallen into a deep sleep, and

The green fog surrounds Crystal Castle

Cackle, the Queen of the Witches

The mysterious green fog . . .

A knight in shining armor.

all of the fairies in the kingdom have fallen asleep with her. But now you can save her, Knight."

I tried to explain that I wasn't a knight. But as usual, I didn't get far.

"Don't be silly, Knight," Blinkette cried, flapping her wings. "Of course you are! Why else would you travel all the way here? Only a knight would be so *kind* and **BRAVE**."

Well, I couldn't argue with the kind part. I am a gentlemouse. But I thought I'd keep quiet about the brave thing. After all, I was once **FRIGHTENED** by my own shadow!

To show my kindness, I asked Blinkette to join us. She agreed immediately.

"Long live the *Order of the Fairy Queen*!" we shouted together.

Tír na nÓg

The legendary land of eternal youth, the floating island of the fairies is a place filled with merrymaking and beautiful music.

THE TROLLS ARE COMING!

At that moment, I noticed a smell. No, it wasn't just any old smell. **It was a hOrrible, disgusting, putrid smell.** It was worse than a bucket of moldy mozzarella. It was worse than rancid fish. It was worse than my cousin Trap's stinky socks. Do you know him? He's not big on bathing.

"That's the stench of the trolls," Blinkette said. "Beware of the trolls. They'll do anything for the Queen of the Witches."

T **as in** TERRIBLE

R **as in** RUDE

O **as in** OH, HOW DISGUSTING!

L **as in** LOUD-MOUTHED

L **as in** LOATHSOME

The Trolls

Color: None   **Gem:** None   **Musical Note:** None

King: The trolls do not have a king, only a chief: Horrid the Destroyer, King of Lice, Emperor of Fleas, Lord of Spit, Governor of Scabs, He Who Does Not Wash Even Once a Year!

Royal Palace: None! They live in underground caves that are filthy and smelly (but that's how they like them!).

Guardian: None. Trolls rely only on themselves.

Currency: None. Trolls trade instead.

Spoken Language: Trollic (They do not have a written language.)

History of the Tribe: According to Nordic legends, trolls can be small or gigantic, but they are always extremely ferocious and gluttons for fresh meat. They hibernate for centuries and, when they awake, they are in terrible moods.

Trolls are brutal creatures that hardly ever wash and have disgusting habits. They also have a bizarre sense of humor and are extremely curious. The only thing they are afraid of is the light of the sun, which immediately transforms them into stone statues!

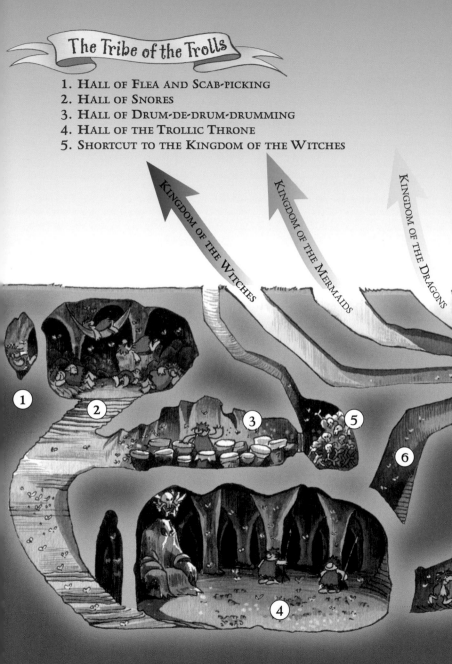

The Tribe of the Trolls

1. HALL OF FLEA AND SCAB-PICKING
2. HALL OF SNORES
3. HALL OF DRUM-DE-DRUM-DRUMMING
4. HALL OF THE TROLLIC THRONE
5. SHORTCUT TO THE KINGDOM OF THE WITCHES

KINGDOM OF THE WITCHES

KINGDOM OF THE MERMAIDS

KINGDOM OF THE DRAGONS

6. Secret Passage to the Hall of the Trollic Throne
7. Exits to the Seven Kingdoms of Fantasy
8. Hall of Slop
9. Kitchen of Humongous Pots
10. Cupboard Filled with Rotten Meat
11. Sauna (the vapors rise from the kitchen)
12. Mud Shower Aromatized with Dragon's Dung
13. Dragon's Dung Depository

Kingdom of the Pixies

Kingdom of the Gnomes

Kingdom of the Giants

Kingdom of the Fairies

The giant pointed at the land around us. The grass had turned yellow, and the trees had lost their bark. "Look! Their smell is destroying everything!" he cried.

The stench grew stronger and stronger.

We heard the beating of drums. Drum-de-drum-drum. Drum-de-drum-drum. I chewed my whiskers. My heart was doing its own drum solo. I couldn't stand the suspense.

Then, we saw them. They popped up from the ground. What a bizarre pack of **CREATURES**!

We spied on them from behind a rock. Oh, how their feet stank!

It smelled disgusting. Believe me

Check out this troll's huge, disgusting **FEET**!

HORRID, CHIEF OF THE TROLLS

WARTS, PIMPLES, SCABS, AND FLEAS!

Some of the trolls were short, and others were very tall. But all of them had big, squat noses dripping with snot. Their teeth were crooked and stuck out. Their bodies were covered with **blisters**, **boils**, and pimples. Clumps of prickly hair came out of their nostrils. They scratched their smelly armpits, which were filled with fleas and lice.

They picked their noses with long, yellowed fingernails. Their RotTen teeth made their breath smell as bad as their putrid feet. Around them flew a swarm of flies, spelling out the word TROLL.

A cavity-filled troll's tooth

Holey cheese, those trolls were a mess! Even a **mega-makeover** couldn't fix these guys.

Just then, a drumroll sounded.

Drum-de-drum-drum!

Drum-de-drum-drum!

A female troll wearing a grimy apron was banging on a pot with a ladle. It was Stinkita, the wife of Horrid, the Chief of the Trolls. "Come and get it, you **foul-smelling** lazybones!" she screeched.

Stinkita took a taste of the slop herself. Then she threw a whole crate of red-hot chili peppers into the pot. "Ha, ha, haaa!" she cackled. "Now that'll

burn your belly—inside and out!"

STINKITA, HORRID'S WIFE

THE TROLL'S SPY!

Horrid stared at his bowl of slop.

"Hmm . . . did you put bat fangs in this?" he asked his wife.

"Of course I did!" she answered.

"And giant snail drool? he asked.

"Of course, I did!" she repeated.

"And **rotten** crocodile eggs, **chopped** worms, and **greasy** slugs?" he pressed.

By now, Stinkita had had it with her husband's questions.

"Why don't you see for yourself!" she cried. And with that, she dumped the slop right on his head.

The liquid rolled down Horrid's

face and into his mouth. He licked his chops. "Hmm . . . you've outdone yourself, Stinkita. This is the most disgusting slop I've ever tasted!" he roared with delight.

The trolls gobbled down their food noisily. Then they all BELCHED at the same time.

Their belch made the trees shake. What a revolting sight!

Suddenly, I heard a little voice. "Excuse me, O Knight, may I help you find something?" it said.

I turned around, but I didn't see anyone.

"Over here!" the voice called.

A chameleon changes color according to its surroundings. Here it is, miming green bushes, gray rocks, brown dirt, and an orange backpack!

Still, I didn't see anyone. I started to panic. Why was I hearing voices? Was I **LOSING MY MIND**? What next? Would I start talking to invisible friends? Or twirling my tail up in *knots*?

I looked down. My tail was already twirled up in a knot. Rats!

Just then, I noticed a chameleon in front of a bush. He was **green** when he stood in front of the bush. Then he stepped on a rock. Instantly his skin turned **gray**, the same color as the rock.

"My name is **Boils**," he said. It was the same little voice I had heard before. "Is there anything I can do for you?" he asked.

Scribblehopper blurted out our whole story.

The chameleon nodded slowly. "So you're here to save the Queen of the Fairies.

THE TINY TROLL AND HIS CHAMELEON, BOILS!

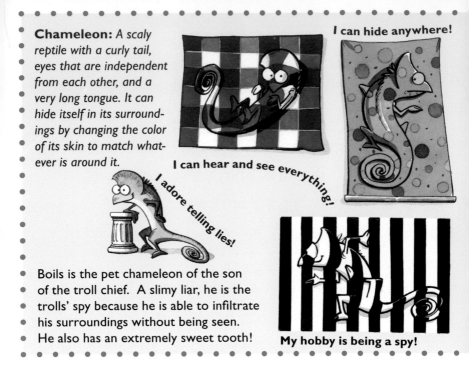

Chameleon: *A scaly reptile with a curly tail, eyes that are independent from each other, and a very long tongue. It can hide itself in its surroundings by changing the color of its skin to match whatever is around it.*

I can hide anywhere!

I can hear and see everything!

I adore telling lies!

Boils is the pet chameleon of the son of the troll chief. A slimy liar, he is the trolls' spy because he is able to infiltrate his surroundings without being seen. He also has an extremely sweet tooth!

My hobby is being a spy!

HOW INTERESTING . . ." he hissed.

For some reason, our news seemed to excite him. He took off like a shot. He scrambled up the arm of a young troll and began shouting in his ear. "**Look alive!** We've got trouble! I just met a bunch of strangers who are out to save the Queen of the Fairies. We've got to warn Cackle!" he screeched.

I was horrified.

THAT ROTTEN CHAMELEON WAS A SPY!

MAKE WAY FOR THE LADY OF DARKNESS!

Within minutes, the trolls had us surrounded. Their mighty drums sounded. A few of the trolls began to dance.

Then, Boils began shouting again: "Make way for the **LADY OF DARKNESS**! The Empress of Evil! The Sorceress of Sorrow! The . . ."

A cold voice interrupted him. "Enough!" it cried. It was **CACKLE**, the **QUEEN OF THE WITCHES**, and all of her witch followers.

Cackle sniffed the air. "I smell a rat!" she screeched.

Drum-de-drum-drum! Drum-de-drum-drum!

Uh-oh. Was I really that stinky? She spotted me in an instant.

"Ah, there you are, Rodent Knight," she cackled. "So you're out to save old Blossom, the Queen of the *Fairies*, are you? Well, that won't be too easy once I turn you all into cockroaches!"

CHEESE NIBLETS! I'm afraid of bugs!

I stared up at the sky, trying to think of a way to escape. It was almost dawn. Suddenly, I remembered something. Just like monsters, vampires, and ghouls, witches and trolls hate the daylight. The RISING sun would drive them away. All I had to do was keep Cackle talking until morning.

"So, Queen, I was wondering, how do you like being a witch? Do you know any nice warlocks? Where's your pointy hat? I thought all witches had pointy hats. Where did you buy your broom?" I babbled.

Cackle stared at me in stony silence.

I'll Make Soup from Your Bones!

Luckily, **Boils** had something to say to the witch, too. He bowed before her.

"Um, Your *Most* Excellent Witchness, do you remember me? I'm **Boils, the chameleon!**" he said. "I'm just a poor, little boil-covered chameleon, but I have been working hard for you. I was the one who brought Blossom your poisoned rose. And I made sure she fell into a deep sleep along with all of the fairies in the kingdom. I did a *good job*, didn't I? And you promised to reward me with a thousand cupcakes, cookies, candies, and other treats."

Cackle blinked. Then she snorted. Then she broke out in a peal of giggles. "A thousand **CUPCAKES**, huh?" she chortled.

Boils nodded, licking his lips.

THIS IS WHAT HAPPENED:
1. CACKLE, THE QUEEN OF THE WITCHES, POURED A DROP OF GREEN POISON INSIDE A ROSE.
2. CACKLE GAVE THE ROSE TO BOILS.
3. BOILS BROUGHT THE ROSE TO BLOSSOM.
4. BLOSSOM FELL ASLEEP.
5. BOILS RETURNED TO CACKLE.

Ahem, where are my sweets?

Yummy!

I'll give you a reward!

The witch let out a long evil cackle. Then she picked Boils up by his tail and twirled him over her head. "You little **fool**! Don't you know anything?" she shrieked. "A witch never keeps a promise. You'll get nothing from me!"

She flung Boils into the air. He landed with a plop. Then he slunk into the bushes.

All of the witches laughed. "HA! HA! HA! HA! HAAAAAAAAAA!" Then they started singing in deep, scary voices.

"Ghosts and goblins, bats and bones
Spiders spinning webby homes
We are creatures of the night
We will fill your hearts with fright!"

At that very moment, the sun popped up over the horizon. The witches and trolls were blinded by its light. They ran off, shrieking. The trolls took shelter in their dark underground tunnels. The witches jumped on their broomsticks and headed for the dark trees.

As she flew, Cackle waved her fist at me. "Beware, **GERONIMO OF STILTON**!

she screeched.

Horrid shook his club at me. "I'll be watching you, Mousey Knight!" he growled. "Just when you think you're safe, I'll find you! And then, I'll turn you into a **furry** sandwich!"

Now, normally, I would have run away squeaking like a scaredy mouse. But this time, I stood my ground. I guess I was tired of running. I was tired of being afraid.

"Just try it!" I cried in my **bravest** voice. "No one pushes *Geronimo Stilton* around!"

I was amazed by what I'd just said.

I *had* become **BRAVE**, just like a **REAL KNIGHT**!

Just then, I looked up at the sky. I thought I could see a sentence . . . written in Fantasian!

Thirteen
Candies for Boils!

We took off after the last witch disappeared in the sky. I was feeling strong. I was feeling tough.

"Long live the Order of the Fairy Queen!" I shouted happily.

Then I heard a voice.

I turned around and spotted **Boils**.

"I'm sick of working for those stinky trolls," he muttered to himself. "And forget Cackle. She used me like a toothpick and threw me away."

SUDDENLY, the chameleon grabbed my paw. "How about if I work for you, Your Knightliness?" he asked. "I could lead you to the Queen of the Fairies. For a small fee, of course."

I narrowed my eyes. "What kind of fee?" I asked suspiciously.

Boils's eyes gleamed. "Well, I'd love to try that bar of **chocolate** you have in your backpack," he said.

I wasn't surprised that he liked to snoop.

Ahem, Knight, I am just a poor little chameleon covered in boils, but I have left a trail of thirteen green candies. I did a good job, right, Knight?

How are we going to get in?

1
2
3
4
5
6
7
8
9
10
11
12
13

"Okay, the candy is yours if you take us to Queen Blossom," I said.

With Boils leading us, we soon arrived at the royal palace of the fairies. It was called CRYSTAL CASTLE, and it was surrounded by thick green fog. How would we get inside?

Luckily, Boils already had a plan. The last time he had come to the castle, he'd left a trail of candy behind him. THIRTEEN PIECES OF GREEN CANDY, to be exact. "We'll just follow them until we reach the castle," he said.

And so we did.

Finally, we reached the main doors of the castle. I gave Boils the chocolate bar from my backpack. He was so excited, I thought he would shed his skin.

"I'll never forget you!" he cried. Then he slithered off.

Here's the chocolate, Boils!

Yum, yum, yummy!

A KISS FROM
A KNIGHT IN
SHINING ARMOR

The door to Crystal Castle slid open without a sound. I took a deep breath. This was it. This was what we'd been waiting for. We were about to meet the Queen of the Fairies! It was the moment of **TRUTH**. The big ending. The final squeak.

We climbed up a crystal staircase until we reached a SPARKLING crystal hall. In the center was a glittering crystal bed.

The Queen of the Fairies lay on the bed. Her head rested on a crystal pillow. She was in a **_deep sleep_**. She was very beautiful, but there was something strange about her face. She looked both young and centuries old at the same time.

Scribblehopper pushed me forward. "Go ahead, Sir Geronimo," he said. "Only a _kiss_ from a knight in shining armor can wake up Queen Blossom!"

Only a kiss from a knight . . .

I started to protest, but as usual no one listened to me.

I looked down at my clothes. No, I wasn't dressed in **shining armor**. But I did have on my best suit. Was it good enough? Just then, I remembered something my aunt Sweetfur once told me — "Clothes don't make a mouse. It's what's inside that counts."

My *heart* pounded under my fur as I kissed the sleeping queen's hand.

In a flash, Queen Blossom's eyes popped open.

"Dear Knight, I knew you would come!" she cried. She wept tears of joy.

The Golden Rule of the Fairies

Suddenly, it began to rain.

Drip! *Drip!* *Drip!* *Drip!* *Drip!* *Drip!* *Drip!* *Drip!*

The rain cleansed the Kingdom of the Fairies. It washed away the green fog. All of the fairies woke up at the same time. A thousand lights SPARKLED around us.

The rainwater poured down on us. No one seemed to mind except for the gnomes, who took cover under a flowering tree. Secretly, I was happy to have a **shower**. Cackle's remark about my stinky fur had made me a little concerned. After all, I am *not* a sewer rat.

When the rain ended, a rainbow lit up the sky. *Red, orange, yellow, green, blue, indigo, and violet*. It was amazing.

"At last, all of the colors are in harmony," Queen Blossom said, sighing. "And that is the secret of our kingdom: harmony. In the KINGDOM OF THE FAIRIES, we all live in peace and we respect one another. Here, the roses have no thorns, and no heart is filled with bad thoughts."

All of the fairies thanked us for saving Queen Blossom. Then they recited the Golden Rule.

Rainbow

A rainbow is said to symbolize a bridge between heaven and earth. For the ancient Greeks, it represented Iris, the messenger of the gods. In the Book of Genesis in the Bible, the rainbow appeared after the flood as a show of friendship between God and all living things. Today, it represents the universal sign of peace.

Here is the Golden Rule of the Fairies!

LUMA: the fairy of light

POMEGRANATE: the fairy of fruit

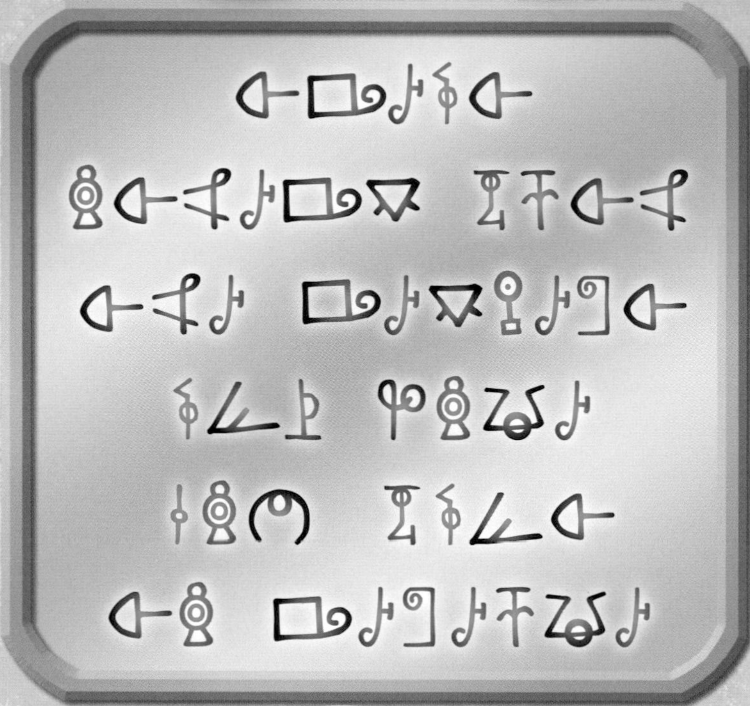

SWELL: the fairy of the sea

MISTY: the fairy who always has her head in the clouds

GALE: the fairy of the winds

RUSTLE: the fairy of the woods

PUMPKINFLOWER: the fairy of vegetable gardens

SPARK: the witty fairy

FLASH: the fairy who appears and disappears

CRYSTAL: the fairy who never tells a lie

WHISPER: the silent fairy

ZIP: the fairy who is an extremely fast flier

BLOOM: the fairy of flowers

SCREECH: the fairy who has a shrill voice

TEARDROP: the fairy who is always pouting

ILLUME: the wise fairy

TIPTOE: the mysterious fairy

SPARKLE: the fairy who has a contagious smile

MIMI: the tiny fairy

SNOWCAP: the fairy of the mountains

ROSANNA: the gentle fairy

THE TRUE KEY TO THE KINGDOM OF FANTASY

Queen Blossom shook my paw. "Thanks for saving my kingdom," she said. "How can I repay you? I've got **gold**. I've got **silver**. I've got an extra pair of **fairy wings** that would fit you perfectly."

I grinned. The wings sounded like fun. I could fly to the office instead of taking the subway. I'd be the trendiest rodent on Mouse Island.

There was only one problem. I wasn't on Mouse Island. I was stuck in the **Kingdom of Fantasy**.

"Actually, Your Majesty," I told Queen Blossom. "All I really want is to go home."

The Queen of the Fairies nodded. "Your wish is my command," she said.

THE FROG'S SECRET

I said good-bye to the Order of the Fairy Queen.
It wasn't easy. I felt like I had learned a lot
from everyone. I hugged the gnomes and
told Princess Scatterbrain to brush up on her
geography. Then I said good-bye to Trick and
thanked Blinkette. I even hugged the giant.
Well, I didn't actually hug him. I just hugged his
shoe.

Meanwhile, Scribblehopper had burst into
tears. I was flattered. I guess he was really
going to miss me. I put my paw on the
frog's shoulder. "Don't cry," I said.
"I'll be back."

the mythical phoenix
with fiery feathers

But Scribblehopper shook his head. "I'm not crying because you're leaving," he explained. "I'm crying because I have a **TERRIBLE SECRET** to tell you."

Scribblehopper poured out his whole story. It seemed the frog had a daughter. One day, Cackle **kidnapped her**. The evil queen turned the young frog into a bird — a red phoenix.

I couldn't believe my ears. The red phoenix was actually Scribblehopper's **daughter**!

"Why didn't you say so before?" I asked. Then

I patted the frog's back. "It's okay," I assured him. "I, *Geronimo Stilton*, will be back to free your daughter."

Scribblehopper grinned and blew his nose in my tie. **Rats!** What would the cute mouse down at my dry cleaner think?

"Fair Knight, I have one more favor to ask you," the toad sniffed.

UH-OH. I chewed my whiskers. What next? Had Scribblehopper's mother been turned into a bat? Was his brother really an ox?

Luckily, it wasn't that kind of favor. The frog just wanted me to write a book about *our adventures*. "I realized I'm not such a great writer. I just like using this **feather** pen," he admitted. He stared at the pen with a smile. I stared at the pen, too. It was nice. Maybe I should ask Santa Mouse for one for Christmas. After all, every author should have at least one nice writing instrument.

THE DRAGON
OF THE RAINBOW

I was still thinking about the pen when a dragon landed right beside me. HOLEY CHEESE! It was one big dragon. It had gold scales and a LONG, LONG neck.

"Dragon of the Rainbow, take the knight to the real world!" Queen Blossom ordered.

The dragon knelt down so that I could climb up onto its back.

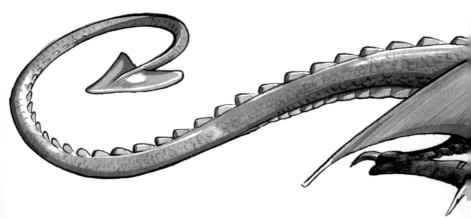

THE DRAGON OF THE RAINBOW

The Dragon of the Rainbow has precious golden scales and seven horns the color of the rainbow. Its nostrils breathe out the scent of roses, and its cry sounds like the tinkling of a thousand golden bells. Its golden den appears at the foot of the rainbow. It is nourished by pure happiness, adores classical music, and is loyal to Queen Blossom. It has the strength of a thousand dragons, but to subdue it, the only thing one needs to do is to scratch its ears: then it purrs contentedly!

Then the dragon took off, flapping its mighty wings. It let out a cry that sounded like a thousand tinkling bells.

I held on tightly to the dragon's neck. We flew high into the sky. I was afraid to look down. But when I did, I saw the most amazing sight. The seven Kingdoms of Fantasy spread out below us like a colorful blanket. It reminded me of my great-aunt Ratsy's comfy cozy comforter. It was so soft and warm. I yawned. I was beginning to feel sleepy. So very sleepy . . .

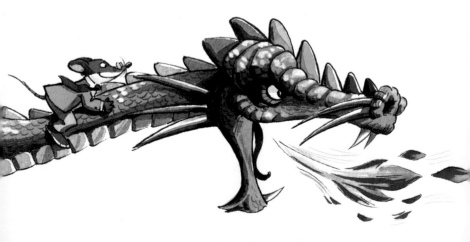

W-WHERE AM I?

I woke up in my dusty attic.

My head **WAS SPINNING**.

"W-what's going on?" I mumbled.

I looked up at the window. The *sun* was shining. I looked at my watch. Holey cheese! Time sure had flown. It was **MORNING**!

Just then I noticed the *music box* in my paws.

I lifted the lid. A sweet melody filled the air. And what was that smell? Ah, yes, the smell of roses. That was the scent of the fairies. But the golden key was gone. And so was the scroll.

Suddenly, I remembered the firebrand the King of the Dragons had seared into my paw. I held up my paw. **No mark.** No singed fur. It was gone!

Was I feverish? Was I crazy?

Was I headed for Dr. Shrinkfur's couch? Or had it all been a dream?

Oh, well. Maybe I'd never know. But there was one thing I did know. I just had to write a book about the **Kingdom of Fantasy**.

I hung a sign outside my front door. It read:

MOUSE WORKING, PLEASE DO NOT DISTURB

Geronimo Stilton

I locked the door. I shut the shutters.

I took the **PHONE** off the hook.

Then I sent a message to *The Rodent's Gazette.* "Please do not squeak to me for three months," it said. "P.S. Yes, that's three whole months. P.P.S. Yes, that's ninety days. P.P.P.S. Yes, that's a long, long time."

It all started like this, exactly like this . . .

I turned on my computer and started to write. I wrote without stopping. I didn't sleep. I didn't eat. I didn't drink. Well, okay, maybe I did drink a few mozzarella milk shakes. And maybe I munched on a few cheese pizzas and nibbled on a few dozen cheddar melts . . . **TO KEEP ME GOING**, but that was it.

At last, the book was finished.

I unlocked my door and ran over to *The Rodent's Gazette*.

I burst into the office.

"I've written a new book!" I announced.

DO TROLLS SMELL LIKE STINKY SOCKS?

Everyone crowded around me, curious. "What's it's about? What's it called? When can we read it?" they asked.

I grinned. Oh, how I love my fans. "It's about a **wonderful** place called the Kingdom of Fantasy," I explained. "It's a *magical* place with lots of STRANGE creatures like dragons and unicorns and witches and trolls."

I started to tell them about each kingdom, but it wasn't easy. I mean, how do you describe the song of the mermaids or the *sweet* smell of flowers in the Kingdom of the Fairies?

My cousin Trap perked up when I talked about the stinky trolls. "They sound like my kind of guys. I always say baths are overrated," he chuckled. He waved one of his **smelly** socks under my snout. "Hey, Cousinkins, do trolls smell like dirty socks? This is one of my favorites. I haven't washed it for a whole year!"

It's a year-old dirty sock!

Glbbb!

What a delightful sweet scent!

Sniff!

I tried not to gag. Have I ever told you my cousin is the most annoying mouse on the planet?

Benjamin tugged on my sleeve. Then he handed me a *rose*. "Tell me again about the Kingdom of the Fairies, Uncle. Did it smell like this flower?" he asked.

"It did!" I told him.

We printed lots of copies of the book. It became an instant *bestseller*.

I was so inspired by my adventure I even wrote a few songs about it. I asked some of my friends to help me. We went to a recording studio and sang the songs. There was "Cackle's Evil Cackle," "Swimming with Mermaids," and "There's No Gnome Like My Gnome." I made a **CD** for everyone and gave them out as early Christmas presents. They were a big hit.

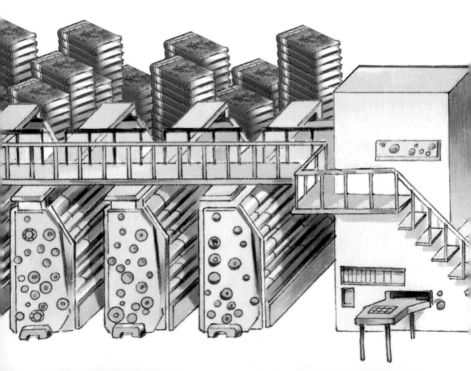

RECORDING STUDIO
1. Hercule Poirat
2. Sound technician
3. Producer
4. Grandfather William Shortpaws
5. Boris von Cacklefur
6. Thea Stilton
7. Tina Spicytail
8. Benjamin Stilton
9. Pinky Pick
10. Shivereen von Cacklefur
11. Trap Stilton
12. Stephanie von Sugarfur
13. Burt Burlyrat
14. Kreamy O'Cheddar
15. Creepella von Cacklefur

In the Kingdom of Fantasy . . .

The next day, I invited **Benjamin** and all of his classmates at Little Tails Academy over to my house. I sat in my favorite armchair. Everyone crowded around me. Then I opened up the book and began to read.

IF WE
HAD WINGS

It took me a while to read the whole book. There were lots of questions. Like, what makes a giant a **GIANT**? And how do dragons breathe with all of that *FIRE* in their mouths? And if we had wings, could we fly like the fairies?

That last question made me think about Queen Blossom. Maybe I should have taken those fairy wings. I would have been a real hit at Benjamin's school. Still, I'm not crazy about all of that wind blowing through my fur. I don't even like *DRIVING* in a convertible with the top down. And what do you do if it rains? It would be kind of hard to carry an umbrella in your paw and fly at the same time.

I was still thinking about rain when I heard a

clap of thunder. I looked outside. It was pouring. A few moments later, it stopped. The sun peeked out of the clouds. A beautiful rainbow lit up the sky.

"Let's go puddle jumping," my nephew suggested. I followed Benjamin and his friends out the door. They laughed and splashed in the puddles.

Above our heads, the rainbow shone brightly. It reminded me of the Kingdom of Fantasy and my amazing adventures there. "A rainbow is a symbol of peace," Queen Blossom had said. I smiled. I felt so calm. I felt so relaxed. I felt so peaceful.

Then I got hit with a wave of water. It dripped down my snout and off my whiskers. Oh, well, so much for that *peaceful feeling*.

What did I do next? I decided to join in the fun. I ran inside and came back out wearing a raincoat and **boots**. After all, I was wearing my favorite suit!

All dreams that come from the heart have wings!

Here is the **Secret Code to the Fantasian Alphabet.** It's needed to translate the secret messages found in this book.

A	B	C	D	E
F	G	H	I	J
K	L	M	N	O
P	Q	R	S	T
U	V	W	X	Y	Z

0 1 2 3 4 5 6 7 8 9

THE END